BETSY WESCOTT

Bravely We Must Go

A. R. Neumann

DEDICATION

To my daughters,
Jessica and Amelia,
who both know something
about fear. Their bravery
inspired this book.

A note from the author:

This story takes place in the year 1900, and the English language has evolved since that time. Back then people referred to Native Americans as Indians. The term "Indian" is a somewhat mistaken term coined by Christopher Columbus when he thought he'd found "the Indes" in Asia. He was quite mistaken! Nonetheless, the term American Indians has survived, though some prefer not to be called Indians.

Native American healers were known as medicine men and women. We sometimes refer to them as shamans now, but we wouldn't call them "witch doctors" as they've been referred to in our past. That would be demonizing their noble duties as doctors to their villages.

For the story you are about to read, I've chosen to use some of this outdated language to make the dialogue between our characters a little more representative of the time period. I ask your forgiveness for my impropriety in advance.

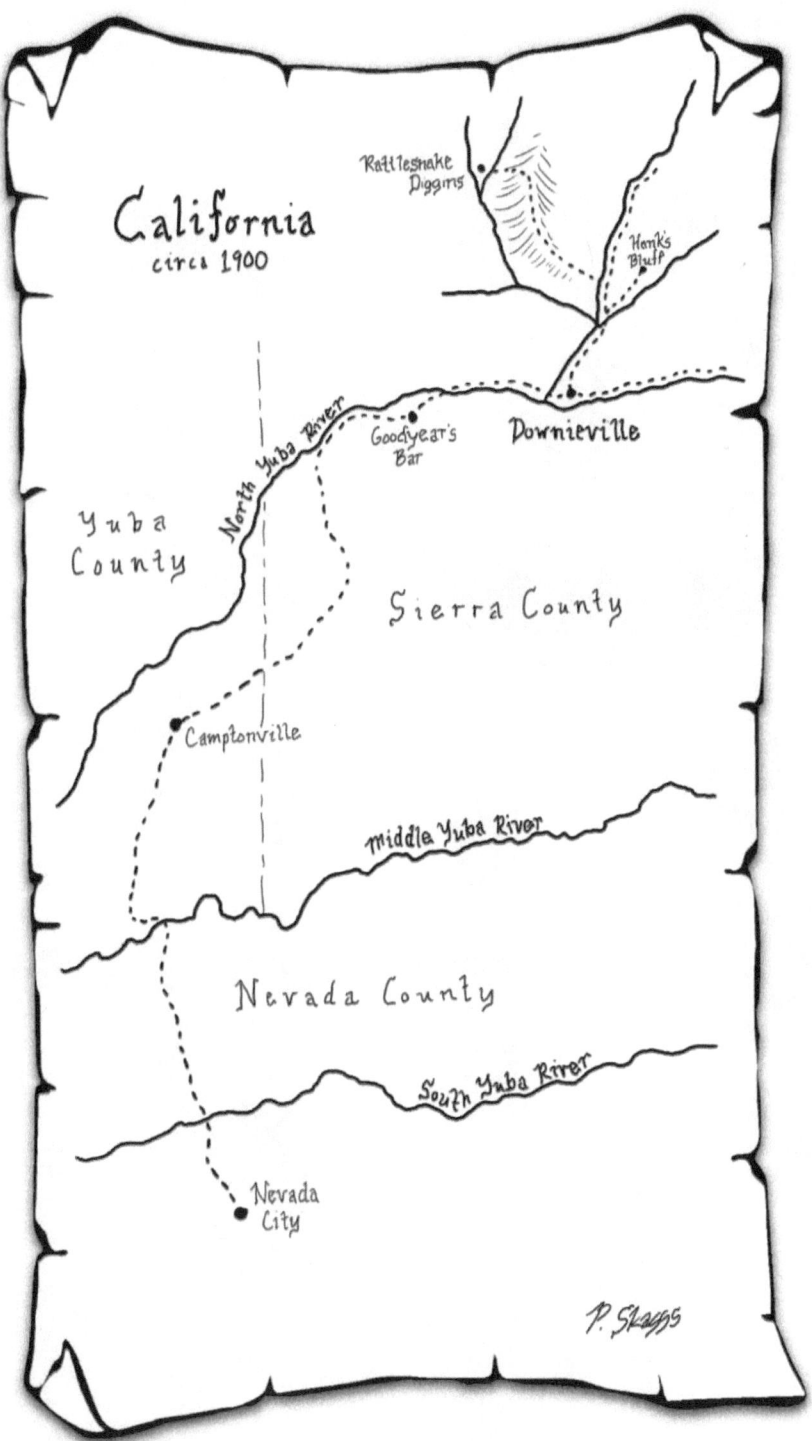

CHAPTER 1

ENCOUNTER IN THE HIGH SIERRAS

§

Two riders spurred their horses up a steep incline to the top of a ridge deep in the Sierra backcountry. The first was a young girl with shoulder-length scraggily blonde hair, dressed in a tawny hide coat to fend off the chill on this November Saturday. Her name, as you've guessed, was Betsy Wescott, and she was hot on the trail of a large bear, though whether black or grizzly was currently a matter of contention between her and the second rider. His name was Jack Fairlane, fourteen years of age and Betsy's superior by one year. He wore a brimmed hat and a heavy wool poncho. He eased his steed, an aged war horse named General, to a stop behind Betsy's jet black mount, a large quarter horse named Sid.

Sid looked more thoroughbred than quarter horse. He had a shiny coat and stood three hands taller than General, who was no small horse to begin with. Sid had a set of blinkers on his harness that rather seemed to restrict his vision almost entirely, save for a small horizontal slit. Blinkers were not uncommon for draft horses, by limiting their vision to the rear and side the horses were less likely to get distracted or spooked in town or out on a wilderness road. But

1

Sid wasn't a draft horse. These blinkers served an altogether different purpose. You see, Sid was handicapped - nearly blind in bright daylight. It happened in a violent gunfight when he belonged to his previous owner, a lawman in Camptonville. The loud gunfire and stress of the chaotic scene had caused a rare neurological condition which dilated his pupils permanently. This gave him uncanny eyesight at night, but incapacitated him during the day. Betsy had made this special set of blinkers to let in just enough light to see during the day by cutting a very thin slit in the fabric. It hadn't been easy coaxing him out of the barn in the bright sun at first, but Betsy had spent months gaining his trust, and now they rode as a team, the magnificent creature relying on the young girl's eyes to guide him, much as she'd relied on his eyes that dreadful night of the robbery on the road to Sierra City.

Both horses were now breathing heavy from the climb up to the ridge. Betsy jumped down from Sid, landing softly on her feet. She crouched and peered down at a few slight indentations in the sandy earth.

"It's a black bear for sure," she said to Jack, still in the saddle.

"No way. I keep telling you it's too big for a black. That's a grizzly," he contested.

"This is the clearest print yet. See the claw spacing? It's close to the front pads, that means black bear. A BIG black bear. I bet my life on it."

"Let's hope it doesn't come to that," replied Jack. He was scanning the landscape below and above for any signs of wildlife. They'd set out that morning to hunt, though neither had much experience hunting. But Jack had been given a rifle by his father, and he'd been wanting to put it to use as his father had instructed him back home. And Betsy had been studying animal tracks, so a hunt seemed like a good way to test themselves. Besides, winter was close at hand and their families could always use more meat and another warm pelt before the heavy snows came that blanketed their little mountain town.

"The tracks lead over the ridge and down into that gulley," Betsy pointed out.

"Let's head back, we're too far from town to drag anything back I'd shoot anyway. We ain't gonna field dress it, and there ain't no way we could get a bear all the way back over this terrain. I don't really want to shoot one anyway - Dad says unless you hit them in just the right spot, they'll hardly feel it and come after you."

"But we could be close!" Betsy said excitedly. "I bet these tracks were left today – you don't need to shoot her, let's just find her! What if it's the world's largest black bear?"

"You want to go down in that gulch, where we're hemmed in on all sides, and see if we can spot - and most likely aggravate - the world's largest black bear?"

"Yeah!"

Jack doubted they were close, bears could get around quickly and there was no telling how old the tracks were. If the bear were close, it would have heard them coming and taken off by now. It was probably long gone.

Betsy hiked her foot up into a stirrup and hoisted herself onto

Sid. She clicked her tongue and gave him a nudge, and before Jack could put a stop to it Betsy was headed off down the slope into the gulch. He shook his head and eased General down the trail after her.

Sid made his way cautiously down the sandy decline between high slabs of granite and manzanita shrubs. The gulley wound around to the right and levelled out little, allowing Jack to catch up. Betsy again dismounted to check for tracks and looked back to see an agitated General giving Jack some trouble, stamping his hooves and rearing away from her and Sid. Jack had gone white as sheet. Then she realized that they'd seen something she and Sid hadn't.

Had it been just a black bear, Betsy would have been gleefully fascinated. Had it been the world's largest black bear, she would have been fascinated and perhaps a bit anxious, depending on its proximity. But an elderly native woman sitting on the back of a huge black bear caught her completely off guard. The woman had white paint on the lower half of her face and tattooed lines stretched from the corners of her mouth, giving her a haunting appearance. There was a fierceness in her eyes that, combined with the face paint, froze Betsy with fear. Sitting as she was on top of a bear with gruesome red paint around its muzzle and other strange markings on its flanks was enough to cause her legs to lock stiff, her stomach to tighten into a knot, and her heart to pound as if it were going to explode. She couldn't move, she could only stare in utter terror.

Behind her, Jack had tried to pull his rifle out from the saddle, but General had turned so swiftly to retreat that he'd nearly been thrown, and now he was bolting back out of the gulley. Jack, not sure what to do, jumped from General and rolled away from his stamping hooves. He quickly looked to check on Betsy and got to his feet.

What was she doing? Why didn't she run? Something was wrong...she stood like a statue!

"Betsy, run!" he screamed. "Betsy!"

But instead of running, she collapsed to her knees.

Sid had now sensed that something was very amiss, even if he couldn't see it for himself. He was backing out of the gulley clumsily, bumping in rocks, shaking his head, maddened by his blinkers, and working himself into a blind panic.

Jack ran over to Sid and tried to calm him. "It's alright boy, take it easy," he reassured him, but he was having nothing of it. Sid turned and must have caught sight of General through the narrow slits and followed suit.

With Sid now behind him, Jack was left with his friend on her knees and the impossible sight of an angry-eyed medicine woman on the back of a huge black bear, slowly lumbering towards Betsy with intentions to do who knows what. The woman's posture was proud as she glared down menacingly at Betsy. It looked as if she was going to cast a curse on them. Everything about her was strange and alien, from the prairie hawk feathers in her hair to the robe of curled rabbit pelts.

Jack and the woman on her bear were now approaching Betsy from opposite sides. Jack moved cautiously, keeping his eye on the medicine woman.

"Betsy, come on," he whispered. "Betsy!"

When he was near enough, he put his hand on her shoulder to coax her away. She was as rigid as stone. A horrible thought suddenly jumped into Jack's mind: what if the medicine woman did have some kind of supernatural power and she'd already cast a curse on his friend!

The bear was close to both of them now, its huge painted head just feet from Betsy, so close she could feel its hot breath. It inched closer, nostrils flaring at is sniffed at her. Every muscle in Betsy was still locked stiff, as if her very blood was seized with terrible fear. She couldn't even close her eyes. Then the bear exposed its horrible teeth and grunted, and in that moment, as bear slobber splattered on her coat, the cord of courage that had so strongly bound together Betsy Wescott's brave spirit snapped.

Without warning, the woman on the bear began to speak in her native tongue. Her voice was deep and strong, though the words she spoke were indecipherable to Jack and Betsy.

"HAY'LIN KO Y'JN!"

With those odd sounding syllables, she turned the giant bear around, and they slowly began ambling away. She spoke again without turning, this time yelling:

"E'MULI JA K'UMMENI Y'JN!"

The strange words sounded like a warning, and it was enough to cause Betsy to go limp and collapse. She began sobbing, tears rolling down her cheeks and onto the ground.

Jack got down next to her, put his arm around her, and tried to comfort her, "It's okay, they're leaving, it's going to be okay - Betsy,

6

I'm here, everything's going to be okay." But she could only lay there with her head down, and sob.

Jack was not a particularly brave boy, not compared to Betsy at least, but seeing his friend in danger had summoned a remarkable courage from deep within him. He knelt next to his friend for long time after the woman and her bear had left, consoling her and encouraging her, but Betsy just kept crying.

After a long time Jack was able to coax her to sit up. She blinked through red eyes that were both wide and fearful, and checked her surroundings for any sign of the woman. Jack reassured her again she was gone, and over the next ten minutes convinced her to get to her feet.

They slowly walked up and out of the gulley, Jack giving encouragement the whole way. Betsy did not say a word. Jack had never – *never* seen her this way. He only knew bold and boisterous Betsy, fearless Betsy. This was a broken Betsy, and his only mission now was to get her safely home.

When they got to the top of the ridge, Jack whistled for General and Sid. He spotted them down in the valley from which they'd come. It was a welcome sight, for he was sure they wouldn't have made it home before dark without them. As he led Betsy down to the horses, he noticed that Sid had blood on his back left leg from where he'd blindly hit a rock. He was stuck like glue to General.

Jack hoped that seeing Sid would snap Betsy out of her daze, but she only stared distantly, her eyes darting from tree to tree as if expecting the bear to reappear at any moment. He helped her up onto

Sid. She slouched over and let her arms fall on either side of his neck. It could've been a hug, but there was no smile to go with it.

"Well done, General, thanks for looking after Sid," Jack said as he mounted the old warhorse, giving him a pat. "Now let's go home."

He made a clicking noise and General started back along the trail. Jack looked back to see Sid fall in line, his head close to General's rump. He must have followed General away from the bear. If he didn't have Betsy's eyes to help him, he'd use General's. *Smart animal.*

Jack worried a lot in the two hours it took to get back to Downieville. He'd never seen an Indian in the wild before, and he thought to himself it was just his luck that they'd found the strangest of them all on their first try. He knew there was an Indian or two in town, and that they sometimes worked on the mining crews. He knew the Indians didn't care much for white men, who'd driven them off their land onto reservations. And there had been some bloody battles, too - stuff that people didn't like to talk about, whites nor Indians. So they just seemed to keep to themselves. *There must be still some out in the wild, though,* he thought, *because that was no Indian from a reservation, that's for darned sure. Poor Betsy, the fright must have triggered something inside her. When she sees her ma and pa, that will help. Surely she'll snap out of it then. Unless that witch doctor cursed her...*

CHAPTER 2

SAFELY HOME

§

When they arrived at Betsy's house, she slid off her horse and ran inside without a word to Jack. He watched his friend disappear into the house and turned the horses back towards Pete's stable, relieved to have delivered his friend safely home to her parents.

Betsy burst through the door and found her mother. She wrapped herself around her, squeezed as close into the safety of her bosom as humanly possible, and began to cry. Betsy's father, the Reverend Henry Wescott, emerged from his study to see what was the matter and was soon out the front door and hollering down the street.

"Jack, wait up lad," he called. Jack eased General to a stop. "What happened out there? Betsy looks to have had quite a shock."

"That she has," replied Jack. "I'm not sure you're gonna believe it. I'm not sure I believe it..."

"Well, what happened?!"

"We were trackin' a bear up yonder north of town, and, well, we ran into a bear, 'cept it had an Indian woman on its back - an old medicine woman from the sight of her. She caught Betsy off guard. We were trapped in this gulley, and she froze stiff. Got real scared. I jumped off my horse and ran over to her but she wouldn't budge.

That bear with the woman on it came right up to her, got right in her face. Then the woman said something in her Indian language and turned around and left. That's when Betsy fell down an' started cryin'. I consoled her best I could, but she wasn't havin' any of it. She just cried and cried. Eventually I got her up on Sid and we just got back."

Reverend Wescott stared with his mouth open as he digested this news, then looked back at the house. "You don't say..." was his confounded reply. "An Indian woman on a bear? Good heavens..."

"I can hardly believe it myself," replied Jack. "If it's alright with you, sir, I'd like to get back and see my ma and pa myself."

"Oh, of course, yes, you best get on," replied the Reverend. "Oh, and Jack, thank you. Thank you for looking after my girl. That's a proper manly thing you did."

"Of course, sir. I hope she gets back to her old self soon, sir."

Jack ran into Pete when he took the horses back and had to re-count the astonishing tale to him as well. Pete was incredulous and must have said 'now what?' a dozen times. Jack kept repeating himself and finally showed him Sid's injured leg. That distracted Pete well enough that Jack was able to run home, where he told the story yet again. It wasn't long before Jack's dad was headed to the Wescott house to check on Betsy and confirm this fantastic tale. He wasn't the only one, as no sooner than he'd knocked on the Wescott's front door, Pete arrived with the Sheriff in tow.

"I was hard pressed to believe it," announced Pete, "but the Sheriff here says he's heard of this Bear Witch before."

"Few years back there was a man passing through who stopped into the saloon," the Sheriff recounted. "He'd come down from Oregon and claimed he saw an Indian ridin' a bear in the mountains. The boys all thought he was tellin' tales. Ya never know. Called her the Bear Witch."

"Is there an Indian village north of here somewhere?" asked Reverend Wescott.

"Oh, they're out there, but no sayin' where," replied the Sheriff. "You know who'd know better than anyone is Frank Barley. Prospectors have crawled all over these mountains, they'll know where they are. He goes to your little church, doesn't he?"

"I'll have talk with him tomorrow. I'd like to know just how close we are to their village," said Reverend Wescott.

"I reckon we best keep the children a little closer to home," Pete added. "Don't want them getting' into any more trouble."

"Or your horses getting' stolen. I'll have a talk with Jack," put in Jack's father.

"And I with Betsy," put in the Reverend.

"Alright boys, well that's that," nodded the Sheriff. "I don't expect any more trouble. Them Indians keep to themselves these days. They don't want no trouble more than we do, not since Wounded Knee."

The men disbanded from the front porch and Reverend Wescott went back inside.

"Where's Betsy? She talk at all?" he asked Mary.

"She's in her room. Doesn't want to talk about it. Didn't want to hear you talk about either. I've never seen her this way. Must have been a real scare."

"She's not to go that far from town anymore," her father said sternly.

"I don't think you need to worry about that," replied her mother.

The next morning, Betsy emerged silently from her room and had breakfast without a word. She and her mother walked next door to the little church and joined the thirty-odd familiar faces that gathered every Sunday for prayer, a few hymns, and a short sermon from Reverend Wescott. The folks in Downieville didn't have a large tolerance for long sermons, especially when the little chapel was scarcely warmer than the outdoors. That's not to say they weren't a hardy bunch. On the contrary, they were strong and resilient frontier folk, especially those who stuck around through winter. Over the next four months the little town, nestled in a crook high in the Sierra Nevada mountains, would be slowly buried in over ten feet of snow, as it had been for every winter in living memory.

Jack and Molly kept a close eye on Betsy that morning out of concern for their friend, as did many others in the fellowship. Most of the congregation had already heard what had happened the day before – word travels fast in small towns. After the sermon ended Molly made her way toward Betsy, but Jack intercepted her. "Don't ask about yesterday, 'kay?" he whispered.

Molly understood. Betsy had stared at the ground the whole service and was clearly in a delicate state.

"Hi Betsy," she said quietly.

"Hi," came the soft reply.

"Hey, would you like to come over to my house this afternoon?" Molly asked brightly. "My ma and I are in the middle of a knitting extravaganza – mitts, blankets, you name it. Christmas is comin' ya' know! We must have two tons of yarn in our sitting room right now. We could use another set of hands if you're willing."

"Okay."

"Great! And don't worry, we don't need to talk about what happened. We'll talk about Christmas instead," Molly smiled.

Betsy nodded and looked back at the floor.

"Okay, see ya' after lunch," said Molly as she departed.

In the meantime, Betsy's father had made his way over to Frank Barley, who was sat right behind Betsy. Barley worked for the Yuba Mining Company and was the foreman of the mining operations up at Hank's Bluff. He came to church not under his own will but at the insistence of his wife, who saw church more as a social club than Godly worship. Reverend Wescott pulled him aside and kept an eye on Betsy to make sure she couldn't overhear. He quietly told him what had happened and then asked if he knew the whereabouts of any Indian settlements north of town.

"Well, we've got some maps over at the office in Sierra City, I could check those for you," Frank said.

Jack's father made his way over and joined the conversation. "It

13

would be good to know the lay of the land," he said. "Then we can draw some boundaries and hopefully not have another run-in like yesterday."

Frank agreed to look into it next time he went to Sierra City, then broke into a violent coughing fit. Reverend Wescott and Mr. Fairlane looked at each other and gave him some space.

"Excuse me," Frank apologized, "bit of somethin' goin' 'round camp. 'Fraid I picked it up."

"You better take care of yourself," Henry recommended.

Frank's wife Ann came over and took Frank's arm with a look of concern. "We best get going honey," she said. "I think you need to take a rest."

Frank was more than happy to back his way out of church, and soon the two were gone. The Fairlanes were on their way out, too. Jack gave Betsy a caring pat on the shoulder as he left, leaving only the Wescotts in the little chapel.

"Can we go now?" Betsy asked sullenly.

"Sure honey," her ma replied, putting her arm around her. She gave Betsy's father a worried look. Her parents had never seen her so quiet and withdrawn.

As Jack and his family walked home from the little chapel, his father said, "Junior, you reckon you could show me back to the place where you ran into this Indian woman?"

"Sure, I can get us back there," he replied. He didn't like the thought of venturing back that way on his own, but going with his pa was a different matter entirely.

"I'm thinking about asking Mr. Skaggs if he might want to take the horses up that way this afternoon and see what we can see," his pa said.

"You want to look for their village?" asked Jack, excited by the prospect of an adventure with his dad.

"Maybe. I reckon Mr. Barley's maps will be outdated, so I think a scouting mission is in order. You up for it son?"

"Yeah!" Jack responded, unsuccessfully trying to hide his enthusiasm.

So Jack and his dad headed over the bridge toward Pete Skagg's place while Mrs. Fairlane continued home. They agreed to stop by the house on the way out of town to change clothes and pick up a packed lunch that she'd prepare.

They knocked on Pete's door and he shortly answered. Jack's father, whose name was also Jack, chatted with Pete about their mission and Pete agreed. It seemed everyone was a little on edge since the encounter, and the nature of men is such that they always feel as though they need to be doing *something* in situations like these. Pete went back inside to grab his hat and emerged moments later carrying his shotgun. They went back into the barn and saddled up the General, Top Hat, and Sally Sue. Jack would have to ride Sally Sue this time, but he swallowed his pride for the sake of the adventure that lie ahead.

They rode through town and roped the horses to the front railing of the Fairlane home. The two Jacks changed clothes and picked up their lunch. Jack Sr. pulled his rifle down from the wall, walked out-side and slid it into a loop on Top Hat's saddle. Neither Pete nor Jack Sr. had any violence in mind, but back then it was only sensible to pack a gun along when venturing out into the wilderness of the fron-tier, home of mountain lions and grizzly bears.

Betsy had spent the afternoon knitting at Molly's house. Molly and her mother had done their best to make light conversation, but Betsy wasn't in the mood for talking. After they'd each made a pair of socks from grey wool yarn, Betsy had returned home and retreated into her bedroom.

There was a knock on her door and it eased open. Her father poked his head in and said, "I spoke to Mr. Barley and he's going to check his maps next time he goes to the office. He thinks they might show where the Indian settlements are. Thought it would be good to know. Sheriff said he wouldn't expect any trouble from them regard-less, so there's nothing to worry about."

Her father had hoped to brighten her mood, but Betsy only nod-ded.

"I find that reading often clears my mind. Why don't you look at Psalm 23?" he said, placing a Bible on her dresser.

"I know that one, Dad," she said sullenly.

"Well then, reread it. It's good to meditate on the scriptures."

Betsy moaned, flopped back into her bed, and recited rather flip-pantly, "Yea, though I walk through the valley of the shadow of death, I will fear no evil, for though art with me…"

"Betsy," her father interrupted, "you should not treat the scriptures irreverently." He came and sat down on the bed next to her. "Are you afraid?"

Betsy wasn't expecting this question, and she suddenly found unwelcome tears welling up in her eyes.

"That's alright, it's okay to be afraid. You know I was afraid when I went to give that sermon at the mining camp," her father said, referring to the gold heist ordeal of that past summer, which hopefully you've already read about. "I prayed about it but it didn't make much difference. Turned out alright though. Seems your situation turned out alright too. If that Indian woman wanted to hurt you, she well could have, but she didn't. Maybe she didn't mean any harm, or maybe God protected you, but either way we ought to be grateful."

"She looked at me, dad," Betsy said quietly, "she looked at me and she had this terrible look in her eyes. Like she hated me. And then that bear, it was so big…so close…" Betsy started to cry.

Her father leaned down and put his arm around her.

"Whatever evil was inside her heart, I know a goodness that is greater," her pa said tenderly. "And He is inside your heart."

CHAPTER 3

RATTLESNAKE DIGGINS

§

Pete, Jack Jr. and Jack Sr. rode north with their collars turned up to fend off the chilly wind from the west. They travelled on the road out of Downieville that led up to Hank's Bluff, where the miners were re-excavating an old mine. A rather unscrupulous little Irish man named Clancy had made a lucky strike after he'd been lured there by the "Bearfoot Bandit," who'd planned to turn him over to the authorities for attempted robbery. Nothing went to plan that day, and yet everything had worked out for the better, including for Betsy "Bearfoot" Wescott, who got away unscathed and unidentified, though I need not tell you since I'm sure you've already read about it. What I do need to tell you is what Pete and the Fairlanes found once they'd left the road and travelled a good way up the ridge.

Sierra county California, where Downieville lies nestled neatly in the Sierra Nevada mountains, was one of the destinations of the great gold rush in the 1850's. Prospectors from all over the country flocked in droves and began digging up the mountains and sifting the river beds in search of that precious yellow metal. However, there were fifty times as many mines and "diggins" as there were rich men.

The mountains were littered with abandoned mine shafts, some of which were no more than holes in the ground now, dangerous holes in fact, or ramshackle structures on the verge of cave-in. Old camp sites could be found situated on what level ground was offered by the mountains, usually by rivers and creeks.

One such site was Rattlesnake Diggins, which lay in the valley that the three horseback riders now gazed upon from a ridge high above. Except Rattlesnake Diggins was not abandoned. Faint wisps of smoke wafted eastward from a handful of huts made from felled young trees and large branches, bound together with earth. In the middle of the dozen or so dwelling huts was a larger hut, half sub-merged in the earth but made of the same construction. The little village sat peacefully on a flat spit of land where Rattlesnake Creek joined with another, smaller creek. It was a curious site for the three Downieville men, none of whom had ever seen a native American village before.

The natives that lived there were called Maidu (pronounced 'My-doo'), and they were part of a larger population of Nisenan people that had lived in the Sierras for hundreds of years. They were a peace-ful people for the most part, hunting, foraging, crafting, and trading, as most native people had for generations. Their numbers had dwin-dled as the European settlers had come from the east, claiming the land as their own with the United States military as their backup, quelling any dissent the native people might raise.

Here at Rattlesnake Diggins ten Maidu families had decided to settle for a time. They were a nomadic people, following good hunting grounds and trading opportunities. Most tribes were led by male elders and some had a respected medicine man – or woman – who was seen to have special power to access the spiritual realm in order to heal sickness or change the weather – essential needs for their survival.

The native Americans were a religious people in this sense, with their own set of unique beliefs concerning the spiritual realm. They had their own creation stories passed down over generations, and they believed in great spiritual forces which governed the sun and the moon and the weather. The Maidu believed in a benevolent creator god who had a mischief making companion in the form of a Coyote. They believed a great snake named Hiki had formed the river valleys long ago, and had their own sacred sites, like Stringtown Mountain and Bald Rock, which were just a few hours north on foot. They had their own annual ceremonies when they would gather in the big hut and dance and sing and chant in celebration or to win favor with the spirits. To see such a scene would feel as foreign to you and me as it would be for a native American, dressed in nothing but a loin cloth and a few feathers, would feel showing up at your Sunday morning church service. What was normal for them was quite abnormal for us, and what is normal for us would have been quite abnormal for them.

There were also many stories that had been passed around the frontier about native Americans stealing horses, getting into drunken fights, and even raiding villages and wagon convoys. Some stories were true, some were false, and almost all of them were exaggerated in one way or another. Rarely did one hear a good story about the many times native Americans had given aid to white-skinned folks when they needed help. No, it seemed to be only the bad news that made the rounds. So as you might have guessed, it was common for the white settlers of the West to have a rather unfavorable opinion of the native people.

Case in point was Jack Sr. who, surveying the little village in the valley below, displayed the animosity such unfavorable opinions can fester.

"Savages," he muttered. "Imagine living in a dirty little stick hut like that!"

Little did he know that the native dwellings were warmer in the winter and cooler in the summer then their timber framed homes back in Downieville. Not only that, but they were easy to build, cost nothing, and perfectly suited the needs of the people that built them.

"Well, I'd say we found what we were lookin' for. Best not to let anyone venture into these parts," continued Jack Sr.

Below they could see a few native women huddled over big bowls, grinding acorns into a fine grain they'd use for cooking.

"If we can see them, then they can see us. I reckon we clear on out and head back," said Pete. "Plus, them clouds yonder look like they might be planning on givin' us an early snow." They wheeled their horses around and began back the way they'd come.

"Where were all the men?" asked Jack Jr. as the horses ambled slowly down the ridge.

21

"That's why we ain't stickin' round," said his father. "They're probably off hunting, and I don't wanna run into them by mistake. No tellin' what they'd do. We best just steer clear – they can do their thing and we can do ours. I'm half in a mind to write a letter to the Army and let them know they're here. Wouldn't take much to run 'em off."

"They ain't all bad folks, Jack," objected Pete. "I've traded with them down in Camptonville and they're as honest as the next man. I never known one to raise a fuss or cause any trouble."

"Well you're one of the lucky ones," returned Jack Sr. Jack Jr. had never given much thought to native Americans until the day before, and he wasn't sure what to think.

"You reckon the Bear Witch is down there?" he asked.

"Probably," muttered his father, but Pete again objected.

"I can't imagine an old woman on a bear walkin' through a little village like that, she may be a loner. You can bet they know who she is though. Might even use her doctorin' skills. That's what a medicine woman is, ya know," Pete said to Jack Jr.

"That's a stretch," inserted Jack Sr. "Bunch of black magic and witchcraft, doin' the devil's business from what I've heard."

"I've heard some of them Indian remedies work," put in Pete.

"Well, after yesterday, I'd say witchcraft is exactly what I saw," said Jack Jr. Having heard Pete and his dad go back and forth, he'd decided to side with his pa. "I don't know what that old woman said, but it half sounded like a curse to me, and Betsy ain't been right since."

His father began to get animated at this, his voice raising, "I ain't one to believe in witchcraft, but I do believe in the devil, and if that woman's done stuck a demon on lil' Betsy, then they'll be hell to pay!"

"Let's not jump to conclusions boys," said Pete, trying to calm Jack Sr. down. "I'm sure she'll be alright, just give her a few days for the shock to wear off."

Jack Sr. grunted in reply while his son set his chin and narrowed his eyes. The younger let his dad's sentiments echo in his mind. *That old witch better not have done somethin' to Besty, or there's gonna be hell to pay...*

It took them an hour or so to get back to the road, and in that time the wind had picked up and now nipped at their noses with a cold bite. But rather than double time it back to Downieville, they ran into Doctor Marten, who was walking back to town in a hurry.

"Mr. Skaggs, Mr. Fairlane, young Jack," he said, tipping his hat. "I'm sure glad to see you."

"What's the matter, Doc?" asked Pete.

"I've just been up to Hank's Bluff by Mr. Barley's request and there's an outbreak of the fever among the men. Something frightful I'm afraid, they're down and out. Camp looks like a hospital ward. I was just on my way back to gather some instruments and medicine, but I'd rather not go into town on account that I probably have the contagion now as well."

"We'd be happy to get what you need and get it up to you, if

23

Pete's willing to lend us a horse again," said Jack Sr.

"Of course," nodded Pete.

"I'd be much obliged if you could," said Dr. Marten gratefully.

"You have a list or somethin'?" asked Jack Sr.

"Just tell my wife to gather my treatments for scarlet fever. And have her send along my volume of Dr. Chase's Household Physician. I seem to remember some new treatment using Sulphurous Acid, but I'm sure I don't have any."

"Is that something I could pick up in Camptonville this week?" offered Pete.

"Not likely. I reckon the druggist in Nevada City is the closest place. There's also a Chinese man there named Bao who has a good reputation in medicinal cures."

"Nevada City is quite a haul, Doctor," said Pete as he weighed this request. "I'd have to drive pretty hard to get there in a day. But seein' how Camptonville is on the way, I reckon I could manage it."

"I ain't gonna be bashful, we need some treatment to help them boys," replied the Doctor before pausing to weigh his words given Jack Jr's presence. He went on in a quieter voice, "My worry is that if this gets into Downieville, I'm quite unprepared to handle it. I'm not even sure of the diagnosis yet. The symptoms are fever, rash on the skin, red nodules in the tonsils, loose bowels, and delirium."

"I hope you don't mean me to remember all that?" asked Pete.

"Fever, skin rash, nodules on the tonsils, delirium, and the runs," said Jack Jr.

"Well done boy, write that down when you get back. Find Bao

24

and tell him everything I've told you. Oh, and Sulphurous Acid from the druggist. And my things from home. Good golly, I'm afraid I've given you a rather big list."

"And with weather moving in. I suppose you need all of this right away?" asked Pete.

"The sooner the better," nodded the doctor.

"We'll figure it out, but it's gettin' late so tomorrow's the earliest you'll see your things. As for Nevada City, it'll be a few days before I can get there and back," suggested Pete.

"I'm grateful, as will be Barley and then men up there. Oh, and when you return, leave everything at the edge of camp and holler for me. Don't come in."

And just like that, all their concerns about the natives up at Rattlesnake Diggins were put aside, and instead they wondered what would become of the miners up at Hank's Bluff. And if the fever would reach Downieville.

CHAPTER 4

SNOWSTORM

§

The storm hit in the last of the daylight. It blew in hard and fast, but once the front came through the wind settled and the snow began to fall in big clumps. Betsy stared out the window in her living room feeling slightly less heavy than she had since the bear encounter. She loved snowstorms and the warm and cozy feelings of Christmas that came along with them. Of course back then they had no way of knowing how bad a storm would be or how much snow would come, and when you live in a small town high in the mountains, there's a certain nervousness that accompanies the snow. A bad storm could leave you stranded and snowbound, surviving on whatever stores you'd stocked up in the months prior.

But none of this bothered Betsy. A good snow brought excitement and beauty to the high Sierras, and a reminder that there was more to life than a strange old medicine woman riding a bear. Snow made everything quiet, outside and in, and that night Betsy was finally able to get a good night's rest.

She woke the next morning, jumped up and checked the window. There had to be almost a foot of snow already, and it was still coming down! She changed out of her night gown, bolted out of her bed-room, fetched her heavy coat, and opened the front door. Her father was outside shoveling a path out to the road. He looked back at her with a smile. The cold air felt refreshing on her face. She looked up and down the street and saw men out with their shovels all doing the same as her father.

Her mother appeared behind her, put a hand on her shoulder, and said, "wonderful, isn't it?"

"It's so pretty!" replied Betsy. The stones in the river across from their house had big snowy caps on them, and the boughs of the pines sagged under their heavy loads. Everything was brilliant white, and when the sun came back out, it would all glisten and sparkle like a million gemstones. But for now, the skies were still grey and the snow was still falling.

Up the road she saw someone trudging their way. It was Jack, and he seemed to be in a hurry. Normally, this would be an occasion to gather up their friends and have a snowball fight, but that didn't appear to be on his mind at the moment.

"Betsy, am I glad to see you!" he said, breathing heavily. It was not easy getting around in a foot of snow, even for a strapping young lad like Jack. "Pete needs you down at the stables. Sid won't budge and he's trying to get him hooked up to the wagon."

"Why's he takin' Sid?" she asked. He normally took Sally Sue or Tophat on his supply runs down to Camptonville. She'd never known him to take Sid.

"The other horses ain't big enough to pull the wagon through

27

this," he said. "And he wants to go today before the snow gets any deeper. We're goin' to get medicine from Nevada City to help the miners, they all got scarlet fever or somethin'."

Her father stopped shoveling and said, "What's this now?"

"We ran into Dr. Marten yesterday when we were…up that way," Jack sputtered, unsure of how much to spill with Betsy present. "He said the whole camp has got a fever. My dad's already headed back that way with some stuff from Dr. Marten's house, but he needs something else from Nevada City."

"Must be serious if he's headin' out in this weather," observed her father.

"The doc didn't even want to come into town in case he spread it himself," said Jack.

"And you're going with Pete?" asked Betsy incredulously and with a hint of envy.

"Pete said he might need some help gettin' through this snow and my pa said it was alright!" Jack replied excitedly.

"Well you better get down there and help 'em with Sid," prompted her father. "That horse seems to have a thing for you."

If only you knew! thought Betsy. She felt bad that she hadn't told her parents about how she'd foiled the gold robbery and got caught after Barley turned out to be a fraud. Her and Sid had fled the scene only after Sid had kicked the gun out of Barley's hand, living up to his nickname 'Sid the Pacifist.'

Betsy rushed inside and pulled on her boots. She grabbed a scarf and shot back out the door. Her and Jack hoofed it back to Pete's, making good time by following Jack's boot prints step by step through the snow.

When they got to Pete's they could see Sid just inside the barn door. Betsy already knew what the problem was – the snow was too bright. Even without the sun, Sid would see nothing but white through his blinkers.

"Hey boy, it's me," she comforted, stroking him on the neck. "I know it's too bright out there for you, but Pete and Jack need you to pull the wagon. I've got an idea, but you're going to have to trust me."

She turned to Pete and asked for some glue and some fabric. Pete found a bottle of resin on his work bench and ripped up some rags. Betsy fixed the fabric pieces over the eye slits on Sid's blinkers, all the while keeping him calm with soothing words and pats on the neck.

"Right boy, you just follow me. I've got your reins, and you can just come right on out," said Betsy, giving him a gentle pull out into the snow, which was still falling heavily.

Sid was nervous. He put one hoof out into the snow tentatively, getting a feel for it, the cold, the softness. He eased forward slowly, poking his head out into the snow as Betsy coaxed him on.

"I've been getting him used to pulling," said Pete. "He does just fine with the blinkers, but I don't see him goin' anywhere completely blind like that."

"Well let's see," said Betsy as she led Sid over to the wagon.

Pete had already dressed Sid in a working harness with a bulky collar that went around his neck. Pete hooked up the wagon tugs to the collar and started fixing the girth that went behind Sid's front legs.

"What a good boy," said Betsy as Pete worked. Sid was still nervous but putting up with it. "Right, all you got to do is follow Pete's lead, alright? He's gonna tell you when to go, when to stop, and when to turn. You gotta trust him."

When Pete was done fixing straps and buckles, Betsy led Sid a few steps. Sid was a strong horse and had no problem moving the wagon even in the deep snow. The narrow wheels cut through the snow and rolled just fine. The snow wasn't deep enough to reach the axles, but if it ever did it would probably be the end of their journey. They'd be stuck. That was why Pete was eager to get going before the snow got any deeper.

Pete hopped up onto the driver's bench and said, "Let's see how this goes."

Betsy patted Sid on the neck and backed away. Pete gave the reins a little wave and made a clicking noise with his mouth. Sid didn't move. "Come on Sid, yah!" urged Pete, giving the reins another furl, but Sid didn't budge.

Betsy went back and took him by the bit. "It's alright Sid, I'm here. You gotta listen to Pete though." Pete clicked again and Betsy led him forward. Sid began pulling the wagon while Betsy walked along side. "I'm gonna let go now, and you keep going," she whispered to him. But when she let go, Sid stopped.

"It ain't gonna work," said Pete. "I'm gonna have to ditch the wagon and get supplies next week. Hate to do it with this storm, no tellin' how long it's gonna last and Shep ain't stocked up for winter yet, but I reckon that medicine is more important at the moment. I'll just have to ride General down to Nevada City and find this Bao fellow and whatever else Doc wanted. Jack, you can stay back."

But Betsy had another idea. She wedged her foot into Sid's girth strap and pulled herself onto Sid's back. "Alright boy, let's go." Sid pulled away and headed towards the road, the wagon and Pete in tow.

"Hey, wait up!" yelled Jack finding himself left behind. He bounded up to the wagon and heaved himself into the bed. It was covered in canvas and few inches of fresh snow.

"We can't go all the way like this down to Nevada City," shouted Pete as they rounded the drive and headed left into town.

"Why not?" asked Betsy. "He likes me! I'm keepin' his back warm!"

"Look, I ain't taken two kids on a thirty mile wagon trip in a snow storm!" he said sternly.

Jack looked up at Betsy with a frown.

"We're not kids, we're your crew!" shouted Betsy. "It's the only way you're gonna make it. Besides, you might need our help digging out the way this snow is falling."

"That's precisely what I'm worried about!" yelled Pete.

"I'm going to my house to get permission and a few warm blankets," pronounced Betsy confidently.

Pete shook his head and sighed. He tossed the reins aside seeing as how he had no control over the wagon and said, "Guess I'm just along for the ride."

31

When they pulled up outside Betsy's house her father, who was still outside with a shovel in his hand, smiled. He was proud of his daughter for getting Sid going, which was good news for the miners as well. Pete jumped down before Betsy had brought Sid to a stop.

"Now I had no part in this and I highly advise against it," he started saying to Betsy's father. The Reverend shot a confused look at Betsy.

"Dad, Jack and Pete are headed to Nevada City for medicine and supplies for the storm," Betsy began. "Problem is, Sid won't move unless I'm with him. So we all gotta go together. We'll be safe as a team, Pete knows the way and he's got his rifle."

Pete was shaking his head in disagreement.

"What, you don't got your rifle?" asked Betsy.

"No, I got my rifle, but…"

"Everyone here knows I can pull my own weight as well as Jack or anyone else! I'll grab some warm things and some extra food and we'll set off right now," she prompted.

"You reckon you can get through?" asked her father to Pete.

"It's all downhill from here, and the snow ought to be less as we descend," he replied. Betsy smiled when he said 'we.'

A lot of thoughts ran through Reverend Wescott's mind at that moment. First was the safety of his daughter. But this seemed just the thing to snap her out of the darkness that had rested upon her since the incident with the medicine woman. Betsy was getting older, and she was already plenty resourceful. He wanted her to do hard things, and moreover, he wanted her to do things that would please God.

32

Helping the sick was just the sort of thing Christians ought to be doing, even at their own expense. *Especially at their own expense,* he
thought.

"Alright," he said.

Pete's jaw dropped. "You mean she's coming?" he asked incredulously.

"Well, you need her or not?" Reverend Wescott asked.

Pete gestured in protest, "Well, I could use her help, but I can
just go on horseback on my own and make better time..."

"...and not get any food for town," Betsy finished for him.

"Well, yes, if we're taking the wagon..." Pete said.

"Then off you go," said the Reverend. Betsy squealed, hugged
her dad, and ran in to get extra blankets and food. She was back out
in a flash. Mrs. Wescott appeared behind her at the door and put her
hands on her hips. She clearly did not approve, and shot darts with
her eyes at Reverend Wescott. He'd made an executive decision
without her, and he'd have to answer for it later.

"One more thing," said the Reverend. "Let me pray." They all
paused and bowed their heads as the snow fell.

"Dear Father in heaven, I pray your merciful hand on this party
which sets out this morning to do the good work of helping the people
of our town. Protect them as they travel, guide their way, and may
they return safely with the supplies needed. I pray for the health of
those men stricken by sickness, be merciful to them, and for Doctor
Marten, wisdom and strength. As the hymn says, how firm the foun-
dation of ye saints of the Lord, who unto the Savior for refuge have

33

fled!"

The Reverend started to sing at this point, and soon Pete, Betsy, and Jack joined in, for it was a common hymn in that day.

Fear not, I am with thee; oh, be not dismayed,
for I am thy God and will still give thee aid.
I'll strengthen thee, help thee, and cause thee to stand,
upheld by my righteous omnipotent hand!

The Reverend concluded his singing prayer with an "Amen." Pete and Jack Jr. climbed back up onto the driver's bench. Betsy ran back to the front porch, gave her mother a big hug, and returned, climbing onto the back of Sid.

"By the way, how long is this going to take?" asked her Father.

"In good weather, two days. But no sayin' in these conditions," replied Pete.

Reverend Wescott put his hand to his mouth as he suddenly realized the magnitude of the journey on which he'd just sent his daughter.

CHAPTER 5

SNOWBOUND

§

All the men of Downieville paused their shoveling to watch Pete drive his wagon past with Jack sitting beside him and Betsy atop of Sid. Pete wasn't actually driving the wagon at all of course, that was up to Betsy, though Pete would give her directions occasionally, mostly just to reassure himself that he was still in charge. Betsy knew where they were heading, at least as far as Goodyear's Bar, and it wasn't as if she could go too fast, the thick snow cover made sure of that. Nonetheless, for the townsfolk of Downieville, Sid's strong legs cutting through the snow like a steamboat down a river was a sight to behold, and the men waved and wished them safe travels. And of course those who knew of Sid's condition (his day-blindness) were even more astonished.

It was a good thirty miles to Nevada City, and due to their late start and the snow Pete had given up any chance of making it there before dark that evening. It was going to be a long, cold day for them all. Betsy wore a heavy riding cape with the hood drawn up tightly to keep the snow out of her face. There was no saddle between her and Sid, only a blanket, which she was grateful for. Sid kept her mind busy, as he needed almost constant encouragement as they went. Betsy and Sid had developed a strong bond over the last few months, and the horse wholly trusted her to guide him, which she did through nudges and subtle tugs on the reins. Nonetheless, it was nothing short of miraculous that a young girl was leading a blind horse down a winding road in a snowstorm pulling a wagon.

Pete and Jack talked for a few miles before they ran out of conversation. After that all that was left was the majestic silence of the snowbound valley and the soft burble of the north fork of the Yuba river through the rocks and boulders on their left. Betsy gazed out upon the beauty of the Sierra Nevada mountains rising steeply on either side and the tall lodgepole pines covered in a soft, heavy blanket of white. She loved this country, its warm, dry, blue-sky summers, the aspens with their yellow leaves quaking in the easy breezes of autumn, and the pristine snows of winter that brought enough moisture to the ground for spring to send forth its splendor in a brilliant bouquet of mountain blooms. These were Betsy's thoughts in those first few miles, and they brought a smile to her face.

Then her nose began to run. She wiped it away with the rough sleeve of her coat. The cold spread from the exposed skin on her face down her neck and out her arms. She had thick cowhide mittens on, but her fingers were starting to ache, and she wished she could bury them under her coat.

"Could someone toss me another blanket?" she asked back to the boys on the wagon in the most polite voice she could muster.

Jack reached back into the wagon and grabbed one of the four blankets Pete had packed. They would need all of them to keep warm if they couldn't find shelter that night. Jack thought twice about throwing it to Betsy and said, "Pull up for a second."

Betsy brought Sid to a stop. She reached back towards Jack and he tossed her the blanket. As she wrapped it around her riding cloak, a second blanket that had been hidden in the first fell down onto the snow at Sid's feet. She hopped down and picked it up. It was a small, grey throw blanket, which she wrapped around her neck to cover her face as Jack had done with his. All the two friends could see of each other now were each other's eyes.

Jack looked miserably cold. Betsy was lucky, she had the warmth of Sid beneath her and his constant movement to keep her blood flowing. Even Pete, hardened by years of winter journeys on this very road, looked stiff as a frozen scarecrow.

They made it to Camptonville by early afternoon, and Jack and Betsy begged Pete to stop and let them warm up inside somewhere, but Pete said, "warmin' up will only make it harder to keep goin.'" And they all knew they were pressed for time.

As they trotted through snowy Camptonville Betsy saw a boy gazing at them through a window from the cozy warmth of his front room. She fought back a twinge of envy by reminding herself they were on a mission and the miners needed medicine. That is why they were out there, freezing their noses off in the middle of a snowstorm.

Speaking of the snowstorm, it showed no signs of stopping, much to everyone's dismay. There was a good foot and a half now, nearly up to the axles. Sid was working harder, his nostrils puffing like a double-smoke-stacked steam train. Pete knew he'd need to rest soon, so just beyond Camptonville he had Betsy bring them to a stop. She hopped down, and they unhooked Sid from the wagon. Betsy led him down to the river to have a drink and a rest.

Betsy looked around as they waited. The road ran on a narrow strip of flat land next to the river. Cliffs rose steeply on the north side of the road. Every level surface was covered with white, interrupted only by the brown trunks of the lodgepole pines and the tan rock faces. It was against this stark backdrop that Betsy's eye was drawn to a flash of red high on the ridge. It was there, then gone - disappearing amongst the snowflakes and pine trunks. She wasn't sure what it was, so she continued staring, hoping to catch sight of it again. She'd seen finches and tanagers that were red, but this had been larger than a bird, but not as big a man.

After a few minutes Sid had had his fill and she gave up looking. She brought Sid up and they re-harnessed him and set off again. As they pulled away, she looked up the cliffside one more time, and there she spotted the same flash of red. It was piece of cloth, rather meager in size, and it was attached to boy – an Indian boy.

What on earth was an Indian boy, scantily dressed as he was, doing out in a snowstorm alone? Her immediate thoughts were compassionate ones. *He must be cold. Perhaps disaster had struck his family. Maybe he was hungry, hunting for food. Perhaps he was lost.*

Betsy had a tender heart, and her instinct was always to help. It didn't occur to her that he might not be alone, or that he might be a scout or part of a hunting party of armed men. Instead, Betsy listened to her heart and decided to do what she could about the cold, lonely boy. She unraveled the grey throw blanket from her face and let it fall to the snow. It would be a gift. Jack and Pete didn't notice as it passed under the wagon and below their feet. She didn't know if the boy would even see it, let alone go and get it, but at least she would sleep easier that night knowing she had done what she could. If her face was cold, at least her heart would be warm.

The journey went on and the hours passed. Betsy's muscles were starting to ache from sitting on Sid without a saddle, and her head hurt as well. She hadn't eaten anything since breakfast, but she didn't want to hold up their progress just for the sake of her stomach, and she didn't want to mention it because once you started talking about food when you're hungry, you can't think of anything else.

The road had separated from the river a ways back, and now they were on a steep hillside that fell away abruptly on their left. The road was narrow and all were nervous that they could go off the edge quite easily. They went along this way for quite some distance, and guiding blind Sid gave Betsy sweaty palms and a rapid heartbeat. Finally the road bore right a little and they left the narrows and began to climb up a rise. Sid's pace slowed to a crawl. He was struggling now, and Pete and Jack hopped off the wagon and pushed from behind to take some of the load off.

"Come on boy, you're doing great. I know we're pulling hard, but we need you," said Betsy.

She hopped down to lighten Sid's load further and led him by the reins on foot. It was sizeable hill, and they couldn't see the top through the falling snow. Jack and Pete pushed hard from behind, and though they were tired, they were grateful for the chance to get their blood flowing and warm themselves up.

They'd pushed for a solid twenty minutes when Jack said, "I thought it was all downhill?" He was panting heavily.

"I thought so, too," said Pete between breaths. "I guess I forgot."

"Let's hope you didn't forget any more!" laughed Jack nervously.

The road finally relented and leveled out, but the snow did not. It was starting to drag against the axles. They'd come into a high mountain plain where the road was less protected and the wind blew fiercely. It was hard to see where the road went, and occasionally the snow would suddenly get deeper. They had to dismount and push multiple times, and each time Jack became a little less grateful for the chance.

Pete had pointed out to Betsy where he thought the road went. There was a bald knob that rose on the right, which they could only see when the snow let up a bit. Betsy guided Sid just to the left of the knob and they struggled onward, closing in on it at slower-than-walking pace. To make matters worse, they were losing light, for it was early evening now. Sid was exhausted and Pete wasn't sure how far the next town lay ahead.

"We're gonna have to stop and set camp on the other side of this clearing," Pete called up to Betsy. "We ain't gonna make it to civilization tonight."

It was a dreadful thing to hear. Betsy's headache had only gotten worse, her body was feeling drained, and one minute she'd be hot and sweaty and the next she would be cold as ice. She was longing to be out of the wind and snow, to cuddle into a blanket next to warm fire with a cup of hot tea, but it seemed that was not be, not tonight.

The knob slowly grew larger and closer until it was on finally off their right flank. The land sloped steeply away in front of them and dropped into nothingness on their left. There was a narrow ridge she could just make out in the snow, and that was where she guessed the road was, and thankfully she was right. Soon they were again on the side of a steep gulch, with high rocks on their right and a sharp drop to their left.

"Right here will do," yelled Pete.

Here? Betsy wondered, *on the edge of this cliff?*

"We'll be protected from the wind and I can set up the tarp to give us some shelter," said Pete. "I brought some dry firewood along so we can warm up. We'll cook up some stew."

Fire, warmth – the words were music to Betsy's ears. She brought Sid to a stop in the lee of a huge boulder and swung her legs off his back. She suddenly felt a little dizzy. Jack saw what was happening and leapt off the wagon. Betsy collapsed down into the snow. Her face was as white as a sheet.

"Betsy, you okay?" asked Jack as he clambered through the snow to get beside her.

"Yeah, don't worry," she replied weakly. "I just need to get… warm and…some food." But when she tried to extract herself from the snow, she found she didn't have the strength. Jack helped her up and sat her against a rock.

"Just you wait here, Pete and I will dig us some shelter," he said

41

gently.

Pete pulled the tarp back on the wagon after brushing off the snow that had accumulated along their journey and produced a heavy bucket and a shovel, the latter he handed to Jack.

"Dig out from under the wagon and over here," he said, nodding to the space between the wagon and the rock wall. "Pile the snow up here until it reaches the top of the wagon, then I can pull the tarp over this way for shelter. We'll build the fire next to the opening here. Should be enough space for us all to lay down."

"What about Sid?" asked Jack.

"We'll rope him to the wagon up front. I suppose we might need to dig a spot for him, too. We'll spread the riding blanket over him and he'll be fine. I brought some feed along." With this Pete started digging with the bucket and Jack went to work with the shovel.

Pete knew from the start there was a good chance they'd either get stuck or need to overnight in between towns, so he'd prepared. Of course, he'd been hoping the snow would stop. Actually, he'd been counting on it. He wouldn't have set off if he'd known this was what they were in for. Most snowstorms only last a few hours, not twenty four, which was how long it had been going on. If this kept up they were in trouble. They all knew it, of course, but no one wanted to say it. And what made matters even worse was they had Betsy to worry about now.

Jack couldn't keep his worries in any longer. He stopped shoveling and asked Pete quietly so Betsy couldn't hear, "what are gonna do come morning?"

"We survive, that's what. First shelter, then fire, then food. *Then* we work out what we're gonna do come morning."

Jack looked over at Betsy worriedly, then got back to his shovel-ing.

CHAPTER 6

A WARM NIGHT

§

Jack shoveled out a nice sleeping area below the wagon big enough for two. Pete managed a third spot along the edge of the rock that formed one wall of their accommodation for the night. They'd dug down to bare dirt and then laid the shabbier blankets down to sit on.

When Pete finished digging, he went to work trying to get the tarp to stretch over to the rock as a roof. He tried various sorts of braces, but he couldn't get the tarp to stay in place. He stood back, put his hands on his hips and muttered, "this ain't gonna work."

Jack, drawing upon his vast snow fort building expertise, suggested they build a kind of igloo, bringing the walls up and in around them.

"We can build the fire right in the middle and leave a hole at the top for the smoke," he said.

Pete agreed to try it and they started packing the snow up into high leaning walls. It came together rather nicely, and in the end they had a rather cozy snow cave with a rock wall on one side and a wagon on the other. They left a doorway big enough to crawl through and then lit a campfire with Pete's dry wood in the middle.

Betsy crawled inside and huddled herself against the rock wall.

"You feelin' any better?" Jack asked.

"I'll be OK," she said, but she looked pale.

Betsy closed her eyes and let the warmth of the fire seep into her aching bones. It felt good, and soon she didn't need the blanket. It wasn't long before she'd dozed off. Jack laid her on her side and covered her with the blanket, bunching up another for a pillow.

Pete cast a worried glance over at Betsy as he set up his cooking tripod and filled the heavy bucket with snow. He hung it over the fire on the tripod's hook to melt.

"Keep fillin' it as it melts down," he said. "I'm goin' to see if I can find us any more wood that'll burn. There's a small sack of potatoes in the wagon. Once it's on the boil, cut 'em up and pop up in if I'm not back. There's a knife in the tool kit under the bench. There's some beans and an onion, too. You cooked stew before, right?"

"I'll figure it out," replied Jack.

"Alright, hopefully I won't be long."

Jack prepared the stew and in half an hour Pete was back with an armful of branches. He set them out around the fire to dry.

Once the potatoes and beans had softened they woke Betsy and sat her up. Pete had the foresight to bring along utensils and they ate steaming hot stew from tin cups. What to you and I would have been the blandest soup you could ever imagine tasted like French cuisine to those three that night.

Betsy felt better afterwards, as they all did. The mood changed once their bellies were full and they'd warmed up. In fact, they felt positively cozy in their little snow cave, all except for poor Sid who'd had to bed down outside. They sat around the fire and began to talk about what they were going to do come morning.

"We can't go any further with the wagon, not with the snow still coming down," said Pete. "We'll have to ditch it here and go on foot. We can take turns riding Sid if he'll let us, otherwise it'll be Betsy on Sid and us boys will have to follow in his tracks."

"How far are we from Nevada City?" asked Jack.

"I reckon we're still six or eight miles away. If it's really bad, we'll have to stay here at camp 'til it let's up. Seein' as Camptonville is half that distance back, we'll have better luck headin' that way and getting' supplies to hold us over 'til the snow starts to melt."

"I bet the sun's out in the morning," added Betsy optimistically, "and we can get to Nevada City and back in a day. We can camp here again tomorrow night and be home the next day."

"Let's hope," said Pete. "Now let's get some shut eye. It's gonna be a long slog through the snow tomorrow."

Pete snapped one of the branches he'd collected in two and placed the pieces on the little campfire. "If you get cold in the night," he said, "throw another branch on, we can get more in the morning." He laid his rifle down next to his blanket under the wagon and then laid himself down. They were all exhausted.

"Night Betsy," said Jack, who was feeling much more relaxed now that the color had returned to her face. It didn't take long until they all were fast asleep.

Betsy's sleep was not like the boy's. It came in fits and starts. She'd slept on the ground before, but she couldn't get comfortable. He body ached and her head still hurt. One minute she had the blanket off because she was piping hot and the next she'd pulled it back on because she was freezing cold.

The fire was just embers now, a faint glow in the middle of their snow cave. Snowflakes fluttered down through the opening at the top. They swirled around her mind in a foggy haze as she tossed and turned. Then she saw two stars up in the opening, or at least she thought they were stars. *Or were they eyes?* They glittered and blinked and turned into a face. There were markings around the mouth, three black, vertical stripes down the chin against white skin. They were moving, speaking, not kindly but angrily:

"HAY LIN KO YI JIN!"

It was half-chanted, half-shouted. The eyes glared down at her menacingly while the voice went on:

"E-MULI JA KUM MENI YI JIN!"

Betsy broke into a cold sweat and tried to rid herself of the nightmare. She rolled over and pulled the blanket over her head, holding it tight against her ears, but it went on.

"HAY LIN KO YI JIN! E-MULI JA KUM MENI YI JIN!"

Something grabbed her arm and she screamed and fought it away. Then a new voice: "BETSY!"

Everything was muddled and fuzzy, she couldn't make out what was happening, who was attacking her, what voice was which.

"BETSY!" the voice cried again, "Betsy, wake up!"

She fought to gain focus through the fog in her brain. Someone was kneeling by her bedside holding her arm.

Jack, is that you?

She didn't know if she'd said it or just thought it.

It *was* Jack, and Pete was there too, eyes wide with a mixture of shock and concern. He was just laying down his gun now he'd figured out what was going on and everything was okay.

"You were dreaming," Jack said gently. "It's okay now, everything's okay, we're here, there's no witch doctor, everything's okay."

Pete put another few branches on the fire and blew at the embers. From the light of the little flame that suddenly caught they could see she was sweating and her cheeks were rosy red. Jack instinctively felt her forehead, then looked at Pete worriedly. There was no need to say anything, they knew she had a fever.

Pete crawled outside and returned with a cold cloth. They placed it on her forehead to cool her down.

"Nuthin' for it but sleep," said Pete quietly.

Betsy hadn't said a word, and soon she'd drifted off again with her eyes closed.

"Maybe she'll be better come morning," hoped Jack out loud.

They laid down again, but Jack couldn't sleep. Those words Betsy had spoken, he'd heard them before. They were what that old witch had said. Now fresh in his mind, he forced himself to remember them.

Hay lin ko yi jin, e-muli ja kum meni yi jin. Hay lin ko yi jin, e-

48

muli ja kum meni yi jin.

He said them over and over to himself so he wouldn't forget. He just needed to find someone who could translate them. He had a feeling that Betsy's sickness wasn't a coincidence. *It was the witch doctor's curse.*

When Betsy woke in the morning, the first thing she noticed was how terrible she felt. Her head was worse than before and she was as hot as stove pipe. Her arms itched. She pushed the blankets off her and looked around the little snow cave. The fire was smoldering and light poured in from the hole in the roof. Jack and Pete were nowhere to be seen, but she could hear someone outside.

"Jack?" she called, though it came out like a weak croak.

"Betsy!"

Soon Jack was inside kneeling next to her. He was about to ask how she was feeling, but once he'd looked there was no need.

"You had a rough night," he said instead. "Why are your arms all pink?"

Betsy looked down. Her arms were pink, and they had little spots on them that itched.

Then it hit him like a brick in the head. "Headache, fever, rash, oh no," he said, unable to conceal his fear.

"What?" prompted Betsy.

"You got what the miner's got," he said. He backed away a little from her, edging toward the little crawlway out.

"Is that bad?" Betsy asked. She'd not heard what the doctor had told Jack, his dad, and Pete on the road two day's prior.

He avoided the question. "The good thing is we're not too far from the medicine. The bad thing is you're in no shape to travel."

"Can the wagon move?" she asked. Her memory of last night's conversation was foggy.

"No, we gotta go by horse and foot from here. Snow's calmed down a bit, just a fine sprinklin' now. You think you can you ride?"

"Maybe..." She pushed herself up and rested against the rock.

"I made you some porridge earlier. Here," said Jack, handing her a tin cup. "If you can ride Sid, we can keep going. If not, we gotta stay here 'til you can. Pete said he ain't leaving us alone. I told him we would be fine, but he's set on it. We all stay together."

"We gotta get the medicine," said Betsy weakly, "so we go. Tell him I'm good."

At that moment Pete put his head through the door. "How you feelin' girlie?" he said as optimistically as he could muster.

"I can go," she said. Pete looked unconvinced.

"You sure?" he asked. "'Cuz it's gonna be a long day. You can ride Sid the whole way of course, and we got blankets. But it's gonna be six, eight hours, I dunno. Long time to be on a horse if you ain't feelin' well. We can always wait it out."

"Pete, I got what the miner's got," she said seriously. "I think we better just get to the medicine."

Pete glanced a Jack worriedly. After a second he said, "Alright then, you come on out when you're ready. We only got so much daylight."

CHAPTER 7

A COLD DAY

§

Nestled throughout the peaks of the Sierra Nevada mountains were many open meadows. In the spring these were delightfully speckled with wildflowers, and little freshwater creeks peacefully trickled through carrying the snow melt downhill. At the edges of these meadows stood groves of aspens and towering pines, fed by the melting snow. Where the meadows rose to meet the mountainsides lay huge rock fields filled with boulders the size of cabins, stacked one on top of another just as they'd come to rest thousands of years ago when they'd tumbling off the mountains in giant cataclysmic avalanches.

But now this glorious landscape was entirely white. The meadows, the trees, the rocks, and the sky, all blended together in a kind of threatening ocean of whiteness. Moving slowly through this sea of white were two small brown dots and one slightly larger dot, insignificant against the backdrop of the ominous jagged peaks that rose around them. Ever so slowly the three dots plodded on through the vast field of white at a pace that seemed almost stationary in a landscape of giants.

Pete was in the front, sweat beading on his forehead, the snow up to his thighs. He held Sid's reins, who followed next. Sid was laden with two large sacks and a bundle of blankets lashed to his rump, and Betsy, who lay stomach down hugging his neck. She was barely visible in the folds of a thick wool blanket. Jack came last, treading in Sid's path. This was his break, though it hardly felt like it.

"Jack," said Pete, breaking the silence. They'd run out of conversation hours ago. "Your turn bud, my legs need a break." Jack made his way up to Pete and they traded places.

"Betsy, try Sid again," asked Jack. They'd all hoped that Sid wouldn't need leading and his long legs could cut the trail. "Betsy!"

The response that came from the bundle of blankets was only "Mmmph," as if they'd woken her. Jack lifted a fold to check on his friend. Her eyes were closed, but she stirred a little.

"Sid, come on boy," she murmured weakly. But Sid didn't respond. The horse knew she was ill, and was just as determined as the rest to help her beloved human friend, but he could see nothing in that white wilderness and would only move if led by the reins.

"WELL DANG IT ALL, you dumb animal!" yelled Jack in a sudden rage, slapping the horse on the side.

"Easy boy," responded Pete quickly. "We're all tired. And we're all worried. But right now we gotta focus. We gotta get to Nevada City."

"We ain't gonna make it," Jack muttered dejectedly.

"We are gonna make it. Look here," said Pete. "See that little

52

break in the pines? Aim there. That's the road. I'm sure of it. It drops down a little there in the lee of that ridge. The snow's a little less here and it'll be even less there. Your job is to get us there. Can you do it?"

"I dunno…" said Jack, gazing emptily in the distance where Pete had pointed.

"You can make it. Betsy is depending on us to make it. Got it?"

"For Betsy," he said.

"For Betsy."

And off they trod, two beat down men, one sick girl, and one strong horse.

Much to their relief, the snow was less deep once they'd cleared the meadow, but it had taken another hour to get there. Jack and Pete were anxiously aware that they would soon run out of daylight. Betsy, on the other hand, was not aware of anything in her present state. She was still draped over Sid's neck, the horse's body heat keeping her warm from below and the blanket keeping her warm from above. Her occasional coughing was reassuring to Jack and Pete – she was still alive at least. They didn't know how serious her condition was, only that she still had a fever and a rash, and she only had strength enough to keep herself on top of Sid.

They came along a hunter's cabin nestled a hundred yards or so off the road up in the pines, and they considered stopping there for the night. It was most likely abandoned, as there was no tracks to or from it and no smoke rising from the chimney. But neither Jack nor

Pete wanted to trespass in that country, and they decided they'd push on for another half an hour with the remaining daylight. If there were no further signs of civilization they'd turn back for the cabin.

The half hour passed slowly. Jack and Pete were both utterly exhausted. The only thing keeping them pressing on was their concern for Betsy, Pete out of responsibility to her father, and Jack out of friendship. When twilight settled in and they began to lose their vision of the road ahead, they brought Sid to a standstill. Jack tried to make out what lay ahead, but could only see vague grey shapes in the dying light. It had all gone quiet now that they'd stopped. Jack strained to listen beyond the sound of Sid's breathing. Even though they'd lost the light, they could still listen.

"Did you hear that?" asked Jack.

"No, what?" returned Pete.

"Sounded like civilization, a door closing of something," said Jack with a glimmer of hope.

"You better not be pullin' my leg," said Pete.

"Let's go to the next rise and stop again," suggested Jack.

The heading they were on certainly appeared to a be a road, but there was really no way to tell for certain. Pete had followed his instincts as one who'd travelled mountain roads for over twenty years, but even he couldn't be certain. They plodded on for fifteen minutes until the snow-covered ground started to head downhill slightly and stopped. They stood still and Jack listened.

"I reckon it's just up ahead a ways, I can hear something that ain't nature," said Jack.

Thankfully, Jack's ears had not misled them. By the time they spied the first glowing light from a window in Nevada City it was completely dark. The snow gave them just enough contrast to guide them in, and soon they were relieved to be trodding in someone else's tracks for the first time all day.

"Just up there in the town center there's an inn and a saloon," said Pete. "Let's stop there and see if we can get a room for the night. The shops are all closed up, but we can ask about that Chinese doctor and get his whereabouts. It's probably only six o'clock so if we're lucky he'll still see us. I'd like to do somethin' for Betsy tonight if we can."

"What about the fever?" asked Jack. "If we catch it, it's gonna make getting' home nigh on impossible."

"You're right. Well, seein' as Betsy's a lady, we ought to be getting' two rooms anyhow. Sheesh, I ain't used to travelling with company. I'll have to dip into our sundry funds, but no matter."

The inn was a two story building with the saloon on the ground floor and rooms above. Jack stayed outside with Sid and Betsy while Pete went in to inquire about the rooms. Jack felt the cold worse than ever once they'd stopped. He'd adjusted to it, but his feet were not only cold but wet, too, and he began fantasizing about pulling his boots off in front of a warm fire.

"Hey Bets, you awake?" he asked.

"Did we make it?" came a weak voice from under the blanket. Jack lifted the edge.

"I present to you Nevada City," he pronounced proudly.

"It's dark…what time is it?" Betsy's teeth chattered together as she asked.

"Pete says maybe six. You warm enough under there?"

"No…so cold."

"We gotta get you someplace warm…" thought Jack out loud.

Pete emerged from the front door at that moment with a grim look on his face.

"Rooms are all taken on account of the snow," Pete said sullenly. "Seems every prospector, trapper, and hunter beat us to it."

"Where we gonna stay?" asked Jack.

"The innkeep said there's a barn out back where we can keep Sid, and we can bed down there if we like, at least it's outta the snow."

"How we gonna keep warm?"

"We're gonna have supper here and dry out in the saloon."

"Jeez, that ain't no place for a girl Pete," said Jack.

Pete thought for a moment. "Ah shoot, I keep forgettin'. Well look, the druggist is around the corner and the innkeep reckons he'll answer his door. We can get the medicine and see if he knows this Bao feller. Between the two of them maybe we can get a lead on someplace warm to spend the night."

"Betsy's real cold Pete, we better hurry."

"She ain't the only one," he said, looking down the dark, snow covered main street. The only light came from the windows of the buildings on either side, glowing with inviting warmth. The snow had started to fall again and they all longed to escape the cold, dark night. Now it seemed they were at the mercy of complete strangers.

They walked Sid with his sick payload up the dark street a little way until they came to a sign that read "Nevada City Apothecary." Pete banged on the door, and in a few moments they heard the deadbolt being slid out. A short, grey-bearded man appeared.

"Can I help you?" he said politely, eyeing the mass of blankets on the back of Sid. It looked suspiciously like those blankets could be concealing a dead body. Pete explained their situation and their need, and the man welcomed him into the shop. Jack stayed outside with Betsy, who was not in any condition to get down. Thankfully it didn't take Pete long at all, and soon he emerged and held up a small bottle on which was a little white label that read 'Sulphorous Acid.'

"Don't take much of this I guess, just a few drops. He said to add it to warm water and drink it down," said Pete as he slipped it into his pocket.

"Blech, I hope I don't ever have to take it," said Jack, sticking out his tongue.

"The shopkeeper said Bao lives a few blocks that way," Pete said, pointing further into town. "Blue house on the left."

"What about a place to sleep?" asked Jack.

"No help on that front," Pete replied.

They led Sid and Betsy towards Bao's house and knocked on the front door. Lantern light shined through the windows and Mr. Bao quickly appeared and opened the door for them.

"Hello sir, my name's Pete Skaggs and this here is Jack Fairlane. We come from Downieville. The good doctor there told us to speak to you about a sickness that has broken out in a camp of miners. We was wondering if you might be able to help us with a remedy."

"Ahh, I have many cures for sickness, come in, come in," said Mr. Bao with a wide grin. Pete looked at Jack and Jack looked over at Betsy who was still hidden under the blankets on Sid's back.

"Mr. Bao, we have one more thing, uh, or rather a little miss on the horse over there," said Pete. "Could we bring her in as well, to get warm?"

"Huh?" came the man's confused reply, then he stepped outside and through the snow over to Sid. "This is a girl?" he asked, pointing comically to the blankets.

"Yes sir, she's sick too."

Mr. Bao stepped back, his smile quickly fading. "She stay outside. Not a hospital. Not a hospital!" he said adamantly.

Betsy's was the one to respond to this, her voice, slight as it was, emerged from the blankets, causing Mr. Bao to jump in surprise. "It's okay, you go in."

Jack was uneasy about this situation, knowing she was not okay, and he became even more uneasy as soon as he stepped over the threshold into Mr. Bao's front room. An oil lantern hung from the ceiling, illuminating shelves upon shelves of little wooden drawers and bottles. The smell was something he'd never experienced before, a mixture of pungent spices and foreign odors. As he stepped to his left away from the door so that he could keep an eye on Betsy through the window, he almost trod on a foot, and when he saw who the foot belonged to, he jumped in surprise. In the corner of this front room, overwhelming a small wooden chair, was a giant of a man. His skin was dark and weathered, and he had long, black hair. Big, rugged hands held a black, broad-brimmed sombrero-shaped hat in his lap. Those hands looked like they could strangle an ox, and the expression on his face was so serious that he looked as if he might have just done so. But for Jack, the worst thing was this: the man was an Indian.

CHAPTER 8

NO MAN OF GOD

§

The Indian man was not dressed as you might imagine. He wore what everyone else wore in those parts, right down to the boots. He had no feathers in his hair, and thankfully no face paint. Why he sat as still as a statue in the corner of Bao's front room Jack couldn't guess. Pete nodded a greeting his way and took no more notice. Jack tried to do the same.

"Jack, can you inform Mr. Bao here of the symptoms Doctor Marten rendered to us the other day?" asked Pete.

"Uhh, yessir. The doctor said fever, rash on the skin, red nodules in the tonsils, loose bowels, and delirium."

"Sound like scarlet fever!" said Bao with a grin.

He's always grinning, thought Jack. *Unlike the Indian, who looks like he's never cracked a smile in his life.*

"But could be cholera, too," the Chinese man went on. "No easy cure! But I make medicine. The Chinese know many secrets the white man does not. Thousands of years of medicine passed down. All up here." As he said this, he tapped on his forehead.

"Doctor Marten spoke highly of you sir. I'm sure the miners will be glad of your help," replied Pete.

"You got money?" asked Bao, still grinning.

"Yessir. I reckon you ought to prepare enough for twelve men, plus the girl outside." When Pete said this the big Indian man slowly leaned forward, turned his head, and looked out the window. Then he slowly leaned back, his expression unchanged.

Pete went on, "I hope your rates are reasonable sir."

"Oh yes, cheapest Chinese medicine in Nevada City!" he said enthusiastically. *The only Chinese medicine in Nevada City*, thought Jack.

Bao began pulling little boxes from the shelves and eventually gathered four bottles on his counter.

"I make for you Bai Hu Tang – White Tiger," said Bao.

"Jack, come over here and remember this for me," Pete interrupted.

He opened a bottle and poured some tiny pieces of root extract into a little cloth bag. "Shi Gao, drain fire." Then he opened the other bottles, naming their contents and describing what they do as he added them to the mixture. "Zhi Mu, clear heat. Geng Mi, stop thirst and restlessness. And Zhi Gan Cao, very special."

When Bao was done mixing his roots and herbs in the cloth bag, he tied it up with some string and handed it to Pete.

"What do I do with it?" asked Pete, dumbfounded.

"Boil it to extract medicine. Then serve like tea!" said Bao.

Pete nodded, then remembered something. He removed the bottle of sulphorous acid from his pocket and set it on the counter. "Can

61

they take it at the same time as this stuff?"

Bao lifted the bottle and read the label. He opened the bottle and smelled it. Then he held the bottle over a bucket behind his counter and proceeded to pour the contents out. "White man crazy. Think poison is medicine."

At this the Indian in the corner harumphed in agreement. Pete tried to stop Bao from draining the bottle, but it was too late.

"Trust me! Thousand years of medicine in my head!" said the smiling shopkeeper.

He cleaned the bottle that had held the sulfurous acid by rinsing it out with another liquid, then poured something else in.

"Vinegar," Bao said. "Harmless. Play trick on miners. They think white man's medicine. Then you give them Bai Hu Tang."

"What do you I owe you for all this," asked Pete.

"Chinese help save white man for cheap! Two dollar!"

Pete pulled out his money purse and removed the coins to cover the cost.

"I'm much obliged sir. I wonder if you might know a warm place we could spend the night?" asked Pete.

"Not a hotel! Not a hospital, not a hotel!" said Bao strongly, his mood suddenly changed.

"Is there another hotel besides the place up the street?" asked Pete.

The Chinese man shook his head and came around the counter to corral them towards the door. "Bye now. Come again!" he said, still smiling.

"But sir," Jack suddenly interjected, desperate to help Betsy, "my friend is very sick, she's just a kid like me and she's been in the cold all day. We come all the way from Downieville in this storm on a blind horse! We just need a place to stay!"

But his emotional plea had no effect on Mr. Bao. "Bye now! Come again," was all he said as he herded them out the front door.

When they were back out in the cold and the front door had been shut, Pete said, "I guess we best go check out that barn and see if we can light a fire somewhere to warm up. I'll see if I can round up some food for us and we can get some of that tea into Betsy here."

Betsy pushed the blanket back and asked, "Did you get it?"

"Yeah, we got somethin' real special," said Jack. "Thousands of years in the making!" He tried to sound positive, though he had his doubts whether some dried herbs were going to do any good.

They started back for the saloon with the barn in the back. Big, heavy flakes were falling slowly again. The main street of Nevada City, softened by the snow, alit only by the glowing windows on either side, might have looked like a cozy Christmas card if they hadn't spent the entire day in the cold. Jack felt like his legs might buckle at any moment. Betsy was numb and her thoughts had turned to despair, longing for home, her mom and dad, and her warm bed, all of which might have been a million miles away. Pete was questioning his judgment and wondering how he managed to get himself into a situation with two kids, a snow storm, and no place to sleep. Only Sid seemed content, perhaps driven by some animal instinct to protect his human friend who still lay draped over his neck, as she had all day.

Then, from under her blankets Betsy suddenly said, "Look," though her voice could barely be heard even in the quiet.

"What?" asked Jack, squinting into the darkness. They could only see windows and the darkened silhouettes of the buildings.

"A church," she said before starting into a coughing fit.

"A church?" asked Pete, not understanding.

"My pa would never turn out some cold travelers who didn't have a place to stay," said Betsy.

"Alright, let's see if we can't find the reverend then," said Pete.

They trudged up the street through the snow until they came to a little white church. When they stopped, Jack heard the sound of a door closing from behind them. He looked over his shoulder and could just see in the light of the window the large Indian man standing on Mr. Bao's front porch. A shiver went up his spine.

"Let's hope the reverend is in," said Jack, but there were no lights on in the church.

"That's the parsonage there," said Betsy, pointing to the house next door. She knew because she lived in one herself. And to Jack's great relief there was a light on.

Pete made his way up the stairs, which had been cleared of snow, and rapped on the door three times. He took off his hat and waited. Eventually the door opened to a balding man who peered out at the three strangers rather timidly.

"Evening sir," said Pete politely. "Might you be the reverend of this here church?"

"Yes, yes, I am, but the church is all locked up right now," the balding Reverend said defensively.

"Well," Pete went on, "we're three cold and weary travelers, one adult and two children, and we're lookin' for a place to bed down. The inn is full and no one seems to know of a place we might stay the night out of the cold. So here we are, asking if we might fall upon the mercy of the church."

This suggestion seemed to take the Reverend by surprise, which registered as a smirk upon his rather unfriendly face. "Well, we don't have any room in the house here, and that over there is a church, not a hotel, so I don't see how I might be able to help the lot of you, though I will say a prayer for your safe onward journey." The balding man seemed satisfied with this evasion and smiled thinly, hoping to excuse himself as quickly as possible.

Betsy couldn't believe what she was hearing, nor could Jack, whose temperature was rising rapidly with righteous indignation.

"But this girl is sick, she needs help!" Jack suddenly cried.

"Then all the more so she can't stay here, you need to go see the doctor, good night now," replied the reverend before he closed the door on them.

"I can't believe this!" yelled Jack, looking up to the sky in exasperation. He turned around and kicked the snow, then froze. The Indian man stood thirty feet away, quietly watching in the dark.

Jack's heart skipped a few beats. "Uhhh, Mr. Skaggs," he said.

Pete and Betsy turned to look at the Indian man, who was now walking up the street in their direction. He passed the little shoveled pathway that led to the parsonage and walked up the front stairs to the door of the church. With a sudden powerful movement of his arm, the front door of the church exploded inward, swinging violently. The Indian looked over at them and with the same arm motioned them to come into the church.

"The door is open," he said in a deep voice while the three of them stared in bewilderment. Then he went in.

Pete walked over to the church and Jack followed with Sid and Betsy. "Stay here and let me have a talk with him," said Pete cautiously.

Inside they could see the Indian loading some split logs into a cast iron wood burner in the center of the sanctuary. Pete went in while Jack and Betsy hung back and listened intently, hoping beyond hope they'd soon be inside next to that wood burner.

"Name's Pete Skaggs," said Pete as way of introduction. The Indian was digging a tinder box out of his pocket and didn't look up.

"The house of God always open," said the Indian. Outside Betsy and Jack looked at each other. That was not what they'd expected to hear. "Bring kids in here."

"I'm not sure the reverend over there is going to take kindly to our intrusion," said Pete.

"He no man of God," said the Indian. "He not chief of this church."

"You mean he ain't the reverend?" asked Pete.

"He not worthy to be reverend."

"But this is still his church," suggested Pete.

"God's church," replied the man.

Outside, Betsy said to Jack, "I agree with the Indian." Jack nodded. "Get me down and let's go in."

Jack gingerly helped Betsy off Sid. She stood unsteadily next to Sid, hunched over and very stiff, both from the cold and from laying in the same position for the last eight hours. Jack put his arm under hers to help her in, but soon realized an arm wouldn't be enough.

"Hold on," he whispered. He lifted her with both arms and carried her up the stairs through the doors to the wood burner and laid her on the floor. The Indian looked at her for a moment, then struck the tinder box and lit the wood burner.

"We best get some of that Chinese medicine in her," said Pete, and he went out to unload the supply sacks from Sid, which held the bucket they used to boil water. But before he got to the door, he was met with the rather unpleasant face of the balding reverend from the parsonage.

"This is trespassing," he said with gritted teeth. His face was red with anger. When the big Indian heard his voice, he stood straight up to his full height and glared at the balding man, who looked rather pitiful in comparison. When the reverend saw the Indian, his eyes grew wide. "I'm getting the sheriff," he said and stormed off.

The Indian made his way to the front door and said to Pete, "I leave now. Get more medicine from Chinese man. Maybe you need it. He good medicine man, but don't believe his words."

"Well alright. Much obliged to you, friend," replied Pete as he pulled the bags off Sid. Seeing Betsy in such poor condition had made him decide to take their chances with the Sheriff and plead their case. The Indian stood next to Sid and patted him on the neck. He looked curiously at the blinders over his eyes, then lifted them up and slid them back off his head. Sid got a little uneasy and stamped a hoof, but the Indian calmed him with a gentle stroke of his hand.

"You trust me to take horse?" asked the Indian to Pete.

"Well...I...he's our only means of transport, and..." stammered Pete.

"I bring him back before sun..." He completed the sentence by making a rising motion with his hand.

"Well, see, he's blind, and mighty stubborn about it. That girl in there is the only one he'll move an inch for..." In truth, Pete was more concerned about losing his horse than anything else. He'd only just met this Indian, and he wasn't sure he could be trusted. But no sooner had he spoke than the Indian clicked his tongue and led Sid out into the street.

At this point, there was not much Pete could do. He'd unloaded his rifle, but he wasn't about to shoot the man after the kindness he'd just shown, and to make matters worse, he could see down the road in the other direction two men hurrying his way whom he guessed would be the unfriendly reverend and the town sheriff. Jack appeared in the doorway just in time to see the big Indian man swing himself up onto the back of Sid, and kick him into a hard gallop down the street.

"Well, I'll be..." said Pete, staring in astonishment.

"Did he just steal Sid?" asked Jack with a mixture of shock and awe.

"I think so," said Pete matter-of-factly. "And I don't reckon that sheriff is gonna help us one lick."

CHAPTER 9

WOVOKA

§

"This here is the man that broke into my church, and there was another, too, a big savage," said the reverend looking around the sanctuary as he came in.

The town sheriff was right behind him. He stood and surveyed the situation with his thumbs hooked in his belt. "Well, this is as full as I've ever seen your church, Mockley! I reckon you ought to thank the Lord Almighty and pass the plate around!"

"This is a house of worship and ought to be respected," contested the irritable reverend. "Trespassing is against the law, and I will not stand by while…"

"So you'd rather turn this man and his two kids out into the cold? Mockley, you miserable son of a gun, ain't you ever read your good book? Ain't that what the ol' innkeeper did to Mary and Joseph? Ain't no wonder no one comes an' listens to you on Sunday morning. I ain't turning these kids out, in fact, I'm givin' them the protection of the law to spend the night in this here church."

And with that, the sheriff tipped his hat to Pete, who'd been standing idly by, turned and headed back out the door.

"Thank you kindly, sir," said Pete to the Sheriff as he left. The reverend groveled behind him, pointing out the damage to the door and complaining, "who'll pay for that?"

"Well kids, I reckon that's our first lucky break since we set off," said Pete once they'd left.

"Seems the reverend ain't too well liked," put in Jack.

"Ain't hard to see why," replied Pete. He went over a lit a lantern and placed it on the pulpit. "Now we only gotta hope that Indian is true to his word and brings Sid back. He seemed keen to get away from the law. I ain't about to trek out after him, so let's get that tea brewing for Betsy."

"You shoulda seen it Bets," said Jack, "That big Indian hopped right up on Sid and tore off. Don't know how he did it."

Betsy rolled over and stared hazily at the two of them. "He took Sid?" in a confused and weak voice.

"He said he'd bring him back," said Pete reassuringly.

"He seemed honest enough, for an Indian," Jack said.

"Indians ain't no worse than white men," stated Pete. "Some folks care for the common good of others, some only care about themselves. Best we can do now is pray to God above that he's a man of his word."

"If he weren't, he wouldn't of busted us into this church," said Betsy quietly.

"You gotta point there," nodded Pete. He'd put his bucket, loaded with snow, on top of the warming wood burner.

On the floor, Betsy was red with fever and delirious, not fully comprehending the events that had just taken place. But she was glad of the wood burning oven that was starting to give off heat and to be lying on a stationary floor rather than a moving horse.

"Jack, you take care of Bets," said Pete. He handed him the little satchel of Bai Hu Tang and one of the tin cups. "Since we're under the protection of the law, I'm gonna leave you kids here and go find us some supper."

Supper...what a wonderful word. Jack poured some of the strange contents into the cup and checked the status of the water in the bucket. It wasn't ready, so he sat down on the floor by the wood burner. With his last ounce of energy he pulled off his wet boots.

Warmth...what a wonderful feeling!

He laid his head back and closed his eyes.

Sleep...what a wonderful...

Jack slept until Pete got back and woke him up. He was none to happy about being woken up, but then he remembered he was supposed to brew Betsy's tea. The bucket of water was boiling, so he poured some out into the tin cup. He boiled the contents over the wood burner then fished out the little bits with a spoon. He carried the steaming cup over to Betsy and helped her sit up.

"Here you go Bets," said Jack.

Betsy moaned. Her forehead was covered in beads of sweat. Jack helped her sit up.

"Drink this," Jack said, gently putting it to her lips. She understood and took the cup, gingerly drinking some of the hot tea.

Jack tried to get her to eat some of a biscuit Pete had brought back, but she wouldn't do it. But he insisted she finish her tea before she laid back down.

Once she'd closed her eyes again Jack whispered to Pete, "She ain't lookin' too good."

"I'd be lyin' if I said I wasn't worried," said Pete plainly.

After they'd eaten a few biscuits and boiled eggs, which was all Pete had managed to procure for their supper, they spread their blankets on the floor next to the wood burner and turned out the lantern. They fell fast asleep.

The boys were so tired a freight train couldn't have woken them, let alone one of Betsy's nightmares. And unfortunately, it was the latter that reoccurred that night. Both Jack and Pete were too deeply asleep to hear it and come to her side this time.

In her dream she was trying to run from the medicine woman, the lower half of her face painted white, her mouth chanting the same horrible chant, "HAY'LIN KO Y'JN! HAY'LIN KO Y'JN!" She rode the big black bear, his jaws snarling and snapping, saliva spraying as he growled and roared. The bear was barreling through the snow like it was cotton balls, but when she tried to run the snow held her like cement. Closer and closer they came as she frantically tried to escape until finally, after much struggling, she woke up.

She didn't know if she screamed or not. The church was dark and quiet, save for the slightest blue hue that came through the windows. She could hear the boy's steady breathing. She must not have screamed, and though she felt like crying, she fought back the tears.

She wanted the medicine woman to just go away, to stop haunting her thoughts and dreams. She pushed off her blankets and pushed herself up onto her feet, holding onto the pew next to her. A wave of dizziness came over her for a moment but passed. She was thirsty and found the large canteen they carried with them, which Pete had thankfully refilled. She poured some into her tin cup and drank it. It felt good going down her throat. She wanted to lay back down, but she didn't want to fall asleep for fear of her dreams. Instead she walked slowly to the doors of the church to check on Sid. The door was slightly ajar, the latch wrecked by the Indian who'd let them in.

Where was Sid? She couldn't remember what had happened...*was he in the stables?* As divine providence would have it, she didn't need to wonder for long, for in that subtle blue early morning light she saw the black shape of a man in a wide-brimmed hat leading a horse towards the church. The scene was dream-like, and the only reason Betsy knew it was real was because she'd only just woken from one. But this was no nightmare. If there was an opposite to the terrifying white-faced medicine woman on the back of a snarling bear, this was it.

Flakes were falling gently and there was a fresh layer of snow on top of yesterday's that muffled the footfalls of the man and horse as they approached. He led the horse slowly, purposefully. He came right up to the church stairs and tied Sid's reins to the railing. Betsy noticed Sid was missing his blinders, but she didn't say anything. She loved looking him in the eyes. She pulled the door open a bit further,

revealing herself to Sid and the Indian. Sid met her gaze and whinnied softly. The Indian didn't say a word. She walked out into the
cold and put her hand on the horse that had carried her through a
winter storm when she wasn't strong enough to do it herself.

"Thank you for bringing him back," she said quietly.

"Must do right thing, always," the Indian said gravely in rough
English.

Betsy was suddenly nervous. Here was a man that could translate
the words of the medicine woman, but she was afraid to ask. He was
imposing – broad shouldered, barrel chested, and a serious disposi-
tion. He didn't seem like the kind of man that wanted to be talked to.
And yet, he had shown himself to be kind.

The man began to walk away.

"That is what my father says," said Besty, and the man paused.

"That is what Great Father said to me," he replied.

The statement surprised Betsy. She knew Indians had their own
beliefs about spirits and such, but she didn't expect him to allude to
God the same way she did, as a father.

"Do Indians believe in God the same way we white people do?"
she asked, hoping he would not walk away.

The Indian turned and looked straight into her eyes. He stood for
a second, perhaps deciding how to respond. Then he came over and
sat down on the step.

"I tell story, you listen," he began. "I from Mason Valley.
Raised by white people. I went to church when boy, learned holy
book about Great Messiah. One day He gave me message. Choose

me, Jack Wilson to be prophet for my people. I cut wood in mountains. My name Wood Cutter, Wovoka. One day I cut wood in mountains and I hear great noise and darkness came over the sun. I fell down dead. I saw great vision of heaven, green lands with no rocks, many animals and fish, and many people dead were alive and young. White man and red man were together and happy. They play games and dance together. God gave me great power and told me to take this message to my people and to celebrate it with dance. He told me all men are brothers, be good to each other, do not steal, keep peace."

At this point the Indian leaned back and let out a big sigh. "I took message to my people and we dance for five nights. Many Indian people come from all over to dance and see my miracles. I told them all do not fight white man, keep peace. But no. They wanted my power, and then they used my power for fighting. Sioux, Lakota, they came and danced, but they did not listen to my message. They fight instead, and they died at Wounded Knee. Now I do not dance. I do not miracles. White man, red man, all man, want to fight. Want power. They don't listen to prophet. Now I am quiet. But I give message to you from God. You listen, do not fight. White man and red man are brothers. Do not steal, do good."

"Just like the Bible says," said Betsy. It was all she could think to say after such a story. Jack Wilson, she decided, was a wise man. A man she could talk to. "Mr. Wilson, can I ask you a question?" He nodded and said yes. "Can you tell me what 'hay lin ko yi jin.' means in your language?"

He looked surprised to hear Indian words come from her mouth, but he shook his head. "Those not Numu words."

"I met a medicine woman, and she told me 'hay lin ko yi jin, e-muli ja kum men iyi jin.' I'm probably not pronouncing it all right, but I'll never forget those words. I keep having nightmares about them."

"Where you meet medicine woman?" the Indian asked.

"In the mountains up beyond Downieville where I'm from. She rode on the back of a bear." Besty said it matter-of-factly, as impossible as it seemed.

Light seemed to dawn on Jack Wilson's face. "Kapam-Kylem...I heard stories of this woman. She is Maidu. She does bad medicine. Stay away from Kapam-Kylem. She is trouble."

"Don't worry, I plan to stay away from her," Besty assured him. "She gave me a proper fright. I do hope I never see her again."

The Indian stood up and said, "Sun rises soon, I must go."

"It's nice to meet you Mr. Jack Wilson," said Betsy politely.

As he walked away, Betsy remembered something.

"Oh Mr. Wilson, my horse. Have you seen his blinders?"

The Indian stopped and looked back. He didn't seem to understand.

"His eye coverings, so he can go out in daylight," Betsy added.

"No need," said Jack Wilson. Then he turned and walked away.

CHAPTER 10

A MIRACLE?

§

The morning light was just beginning to fall upon the quiet streets of Nevada City. Only three inches of new snow had fallen overnight, much to Betsy's relief. It shouldn't slow their journey back to the wagon by much. But with the light came a new problem, Sid had no protection for his poor eyes. He would soon be snow blind. They'd have to fashion something from the materials they had on hand, which was easier said than done.

"We'll fix you up somethin'," she told him before returning to the warmth of the sanctuary. Jack and Pete were still sound asleep. She found a biscuit that was to have been her supper the night before, sat down on a pew, and ate.

What a peculiar Indian was Jack Wilson, she thought. Even his name was peculiar, though it wasn't uncommon at that time for a native American who interacted with white people to take an English name. Betsy recalled there was such a man amongst the miners who also went by an English name. Name aside, Jack Wilson seemed to know something of Christianity from his upbringing, and what was more, claimed to have had a vision from God and to be a prophet and to have performed miracles! That seemed a bit of a stretch to her, but she had to admit, there was *something* about him. Perhaps confidence was the right word. Or maybe authority was the right word. She could see how people had flocked to him in the past.

Pete rolled over and sat up, rubbing his eyes. When he saw Betsy was already awake he asked how she was feeling. She hadn't really thought of it with all that had happened in the last half hour.

"Better, now that you mention it," she replied.

"Glad to see you eating something. Maybe that Chinese man's secret remedy worked. You able to travel, if that Indian brings back our horse?"

"I got good news on that front," she said. "Sid's right outside."

"Well by-gum, that is good news. We owe that man a debt for getting us a place to sleep, even if it was by questionable means. So, you feel up to headin' back today?"

"Well I don't think we're very welcome here, so yes. Except Sid has lost his blinders."

"Ahhh, shoot. That Indian must not of realized his condition."

Jack let out a groggy yawn and opened his eyes. "What's this about Indians?" he asked, still half asleep.

"Our Indian turned out to be a good man, he brought Sid back. We just need to make him some new blinders," replied Pete.

Jack coughed a few times and sat up, "Good. This ain't a very friendly town. Even the pastor don't like visitors. What's there to eat?"

"I got some hardtack and jerky in the bag I left on Sid," said Pete.

"It'll just need warmin' up a hair. I reckon we ought to brew up some of that special tea, just in case. And I reckon we ought to double up our supply while we're here, so I mean to stop back there on our way out of town."

"I'll go get the hardtack," said Betsy. Hardtack was a hard, bland biscuit wafer made from flour and water. It didn't spoil, so it was good for long journeys, and Pete often packed it as a rather bland snack since meals on the road were sometimes long in between. Betsy walked out of the church, and Sid greeted her with one of his friendly whinnies. His eyes were still open, though the morning light had grown a little brighter. That's when Betsy noticed something was different.

"Your pupils, they aren't dilated anymore," she said quietly to him. The full significance of this then dawned on her, and she said it again, but louder, "Your pupils, they aren't dilated anymore!"

She ran back into the church and shouted with exuberant joy, "HIS PUPILS, THEY AREN'T DILATED ANY MORE!"

"What's that? You mean he ain't day blind?" asked Pete, jumping to his feet. Jack and Pete hurried outside.

"Well, I'll be! What happened to you last night?" asked Pete. Sid greeted this attention with a swift rear of his head and some light, happy stamping of his feet.

"Did Jack Wilson cure you?" asked Betsy, hugging her horse around the neck.

"Jack Wilson?" said Jack, confused.

"The Indian's name is Jack Wilson," she said matter-of-factly.

"What, you spoke to him?" Jack asked.

"Yes, while you two were getting' your beauty sleep," she replied.

They moved back into the church and she told them all about what had happened before they'd woke. Pete was amazed while Jack was more bewildered, if rather skeptical. *Had an Indian prophet really healed Sid?* He was not one to believe in miracles, even if he could see them with his own eyes apparently. Sid stood outside in the light of the new day without a hint of discomfort, and Jack had to admit, he was glad for it.

He knew, as they all did, that they couldn't afford to stay for long in the warmth of the church sanctuary. As much as they disliked the thought, they had to venture back into the cold and spend the next eight hours trudging through snow to get back to the wagon, where they'd spend the next night in significantly less warm surroundings.

The good news was there hadn't been enough snow to completely fill their tracks, so the going should be easier. It only took a few minutes to pack their things. They all hesitated by the wood burner to appreciate its warmth one last time, then headed out. It was still snowing lightly, and though the cold was not pleasant, it wasn't the biting kind of cold that would sometimes come in the worst of winter. Pete threw the bags onto Sid and tied them secure, and Betsy gingerly pulled herself up. Though she was feeling a fair stretch better than the day before, she was still weak and shaky. At least this morning she could sit proud rather than slumped over like dead body.

As they left, they saw the eyes of Reverend Mockley glaring angrily out of the parsonage window. This was particularly uncomforting for Betsy and Jack, who were justifiably anxious to put this town behind them.

"I dare to say this is one of the unfriendliest town's I've ever had the displeasure of visiting," said Pete as they passed by.

Besty and Jack were equally uncomfortable when Pete stopped into Mr. Bao's shop just a short way up the road to purchase additional quantities of the medicinal tea as Jack Wilson had suggested.

"I'll only be a moment," he said, indicating to Betsy and Jack to stay outside.

Pete summoned Mr. Bao who eventually came to the door and let him in. As he again gathered the four components of the tea, Bao asked about "the girl." Pete said that indeed she was feeling better, and Mr. Bao grinned widely, pointed to his skull and said, "thousand years medicine, very good!" But when Pete handed him another two dollars, Mr. Bao frowned.

"Six dollars please," he said.

"What?" exclaimed Pete. "Yesterday I paid two dollars!"

"Yes, but now I know medicine works!" the Chinese man replied, his grin returning. Pete begrudgingly paid the man out of the supplies money, money he needed to pay for critical food and sundries to replenish the inventory at Shep's Mercantile. Before Pete gave over the last dollar, however, he held it for a moment.

"That man in here last night, is his name Jack Wilson?" asked Pete.

Bao eyed the last dollar, then eyed Pete. "Yes. Very famous." He tried to grab the dollar but Pete was too quick.

"What's he famous for?" asked Pete.

"Famous Indian miracle man. One time he made ice drop from the sky during summer. They say he is bullet proof." Bao tried to snatch the dollar again, but failed.

"Why was he in here?"

"He great medicine man, I great medicine man." He snatched again, and this time he got the dollar. "Bye now!"

With his bargaining chip gone, Pete turned and let himself out the door and into the cold.

"Come on kids, time to go home and deliver some medicine," he said with a brave face. Betsy and Jack simultaneously breathed sighs of relief that were visible in the cold morning air. They were more than ready.

The journey back to the wagon was easier on two counts. One, they had their own furrow to walk in that they'd trailblazed the day before, and two, Betsy was feeling much better. It was nice to have her upright again, and her conversation made the next hours of hiking, which was still quite strenuous, go more quickly.

"So, you gotta admit, not all Indians are as bad as you suspected," Betsy taunted Jack.

"Yeah, I guess," he said. He didn't like being corrected.

"Good ones and bad ones, just like the rest of us," said Pete to temper the conversation.

"But you don't really think he healed Sid with some kind of Indian magic, do you?" Jack said to Betsy.

"Well apparently this isn't his first miracle, if we're to believe Bao back there," Betsy retorted playfully. "Or maybe Jack Wilson got some one thousand year old medicine from him, and Bao is the one to thank."

"I don't suppose we'll ever know," put in Pete, "but I sure am grateful. Sid's gonna be my new lead horse."

Betsy patted Sid on the neck, but inside she cringed a little at Pete's comment. She liked to think of Sid as *her* horse, even though that wasn't the case. Sid was most definitely Pete's horse, and he had a living to make. Sid would be a big help to him now that he was no longer day-blind.

In about six hours they got to the part of the road where the gorge got deep on their right and the rocks rose high on their left, and they sensed they were getting close to the abandoned wagon and their make-shift snow cave.

"What are we gonna do about getting' your wagon out?" asked Jack.

"I've been ponderin' that myself," said Pete. "I reckon we're gonna have to leave it and go on like we are now. I'll have to come back and get it when this snow melts, and hope someone hasn't beat me to it."

"Ugh," Jack groaned, "that's a long way on foot. Hey, we must be gettin' close! I see a trace of smoke risin' up over that rock up there."

"There ain't ought to be no smoke…" said Pete. "We put that fire out, and it weren't big to start with."

They trod on a bit wondering what the smoke could mean. When they were close Pete said, "Hold up there, Betsy, let me scout the way ahead. Keep quiet." He unstrapped the rifle from Sid and went up ahead a ways. Betsy and Jack could still see him. Their furrow in the snow went to the left around a boulder, and here Pete paused and peeked cautiously to survey what was ahead. He ducked back around, looked at them, and put a finger to his mouth to signal them to stay quiet.

"Who goes there up yonder on the road?" Pete yelled.

There was no reply. Pete aimed his rifle to the sky to fire a warning shot, but when Betsy saw his intention she began waving frantically. Pete paused. Betsy pointed to Sid. Pete nodded. He'd forgotten that it was a gunfight that had caused Sid to go day-blind in the first place. That was after all how he'd come by the name Sid the Pacifist.

Pete looked back around the edge of the rock and then jumped back. A tall man in heavy brown leather coat emerged and stared at them.

"Hey there Pete. Betsy. Jack," he said warmly.

"Dad!" yelled Jack joyously. He made his way over to him.

"We was getting' worried about you. Thought I'd better come an' check on ya."

"You gave me a right scare there, Mr. Fairlane, but I am glad to see you," said Pete with an embarrassed look on his face.

"Hope you don't mind I borrowed General for the trip," he said. "It looks like you might be needin' two horses to get your wagon off this ledge."

"Well, yes, a second horse might come in useful," stammered Pete.

Once Jack reached his dad's side, relief swept over him and he sat down in the snow. "As long as I can ride the rest of the way to Downieville," he said and flopped back, utterly spent.

CHAPTER 11

HOMEWARD YET BOUND

§

Jack Fairlane Sr. had arrived the night before. Now I must pause for just a moment and beg your pardon. I'm sure right now you're thinking just how many Jacks are going to be in this story? Well, we're up to three, and that's it. I promise. I didn't intend it this way, that's just how it happened. There was Jack Jr., Jack Sr., and Jack Wilson. Anyway, back to the story, and Jack Sr.

It was just getting dark when he came upon Pete's wagon, which he recognized at once, and he decided to rekindle the campfire and spend the night in the snow cave since it was too late to go any further.

The next morning he saw their tracks going on to Nevada City and intended to follow, but soon ran into a horse-sized problem. The road was so narrow at that point that the wagon blocked the whole width. The only way around it was over it. Jack Sr. had to climb over the wagon just to get to the snow cave the night before, and he'd left General tied up on the opposite side. That morning, he'd had no choice but to follow their tracks on foot, which he did for a while. But after an hour he grew nervous and turned back, concerned that

General might be taken by Indians, whom Jack Sr. had not much respect for, his opinion being informed only by the embellished stories passed around of the negative kind. Nonetheless, General was Pete's lead horse and livelihood, and he didn't want anything to happen to him on his watch.

Jack Sr. considered backtracking and finding another way to Nevada City, but he didn't know those parts and didn't want to get lost, nor did he want to miss Pete and the kids if they were heading back the way they came. In the end, he set himself on the job of getting the wagon unstuck. If he could dig it out, he could probably get General around it, though he'd have to destroy the snow cave in the process.

Betsy and Jack looked rather sour as the four of them stood around the wagon now. They'd been looking forward to resting their weary bodies in the warmth of the cozy snow cave, but thanks to Jack Sr.'s digging, it now lay at the bottom of the gully. The trade-off was that the wagon was now unstuck.

"Sorry kids, it was the only way I was goin' to get General on the right side of the wagon," he said to them in a consoling tone.

"Where we gonna sleep tonight?" moaned Jack disrespectfully.

"With two horses, we ought to be able to make some headway on this road," said Pete, looking back towards Nevada City. "We'll have to go back that way until we can find a place to turn her around."

"But it's already mid-afternoon," whined Jack. He had some gall to talk that way in front of his father, Betsy thought.

"We can drive into the night, can't we Pete?" proposed Jack Sr.

"We can sure try, maybe make it to Goodyear's Bar if we're lucky," replied Pete.

"I'm thinking we may need to do better than that," suggested Jack Sr. He looked over at Betsy and continued, "Your ma and pa have been rather worried, which is what drove me to come out here. And I'm afraid their worrying ain't the worst part. Your father wasn't looking so good when I left him. Coughin', too. I reckon he's caught what them miners caught. Did you get that medicine?"

"Yeah, we got it," said Jack Jr. proudly. He'd climbed up into the wagon and was sitting with a blanket around him, shivering. "And we know it works. Betsy got sick as soon as we left, she barely made it to Nevada City, but the medicine made her better."

"Then I reckon we get that medicine back to Downieville as soon as we can, even if it means we drive through the night," said Jack Sr.

"I'm due to pick up a load in Camptonville," put in Pete.

Jack Sr. shook his head, "I think we ought to scrap those plans and get back. You'll have to make another trip."

Jack Jr. suddenly started coughing and his father gave him a hard look. "You alright there, son?"

"I'm aching, but I don't know if it's from all the trudging through this snow or something worse."

"Your color's gone," said his father, looking a bit closer.

Betsy came to the side of the wagon and told Jack to roll up his sleeves. He did so reluctantly, and they all saw the start of a pink rash on his wrists, the same as Betsy had.

"I'll make a spot you can lay down in the back," said Pete, jumping into the back of the wagon. He was coughing occasionally as well.

Betsy went over and put another log on the fire. "Pete, we better brew up some of that tea. Could you hand me your bucket?"

Pete did, along with the satchel of Bai Hu Tang. While Betsy filled the bucket with snow, Pete rearranged their travelling sacks, unloaded Sid, and reloaded the wagon. He harnessed the two horses using the extra tackle that Jack Sr. had wisely brought along. While Pete was busy, Jack and Besty got Jack Sr. caught up on all that had happened, including how Sid had been miraculously cured by Jack Wilson the Indian prophet, to which Jack Sr. looked particularly skeptical.

When Pete was done with the wagon preparations he said, "I'll head out and see if I can get this train turned around. Y'all stay here and warm up and get some tea in Jack."

They all knew they were in a race against time now. The scarlet fever was spreading quickly, and it would be far better for Jack and Pete if they could get back to the warmth of their homes rather than out in the cold. No one wanted to go through what Betsy had gone through the past two days. In addition to that, Reverend Wescott and the miners needed the medicine urgently, and twenty miles of snow-heavy road still lay between the wagon and Downieville.

Jack, huddled by the fire, showed Betsy how to prepare the Bai Hu Tang. When it was brewed he sipped it tentatively. It tasted like bitter grass and was quite sharp, but the warmth felt good going down. Betsy prepared more for Pete and even herself as a precaution.

She took a few sips. She was cold, tired, and achy, remnants of the scarlet fever. She wanted to go home. It was easy to forget they were on a rescue mission, and hard not to fantasize about curling up in her warm bed. Neither Jack nor Betsy had the energy for conversation, though Jack's father kept asking questions about Bao and Jack Wilson.

It took about twenty minutes for Pete to return with the wagon headed in the right direction. Betsy smothered the fire and they all climbed aboard, Betsy on the bench with Pete and Jack Sr. in the back with his son, who lied down and was soon fast asleep.

General and Sid strained and pulled against their harnesses, fighting against the two feet of snow that lay on the road along the gully. Eventually they emerged in the wide mountain meadow that had taken them so long to traverse two days prior. Their tracks were mostly filled in with snow that had fallen since then, and now the horses began to struggle even more. The snow was piling up in front of the axles. The wagon had become a snow plow, and it soon became clear the horses wouldn't be able to pull it.

Jack Sr. was the first to hop off and push. Pete was next, handing the reigns to Betsy, but even with two men pushing from behind the increased drag from the snow in front of the axles was too great. Pete and Jack Sr. tried walking in front to beat down the snow, but that, too, didn't work. It eventually piled up and brought everything to a standstill.

The horses stopped their straining and stood breathing heavily, steam pouring from their muzzles. Pete was doubled over, panting and coughing from the exertion. He was doing his best to hide it, but he had caught the fever, too, and everyone knew it.

"Pete, why don't you rest a bit and let me figure this out," said Jack Sr. quietly. "There must be way we can get through." He helped Pete up into the wagon where he sat down in the back and gathered himself a blanket next to Jack, who was sleeping, but fitfully.

Betsy was still on the driver's bench, a sense of dread welling up inside her. *Would this nightmare ever come to an end? Nothing had gone right - at every turn there was something else trying to stop them.* She was still getting over her sickness and she was tired, and now everyone she loved was coming down with the same thing. She didn't know how serious it was, but judging by the urgency with which Doctor Marten had requested the medicine, she figured that it could be deadly. And now her dad had it, and if he had it, then her mother was surely next, not to mention Jack and Pete. They'd barely managed to get the medicine, and now they couldn't get it to the people that needed it.

Why did the snowstorm have to come when it did, Betsy thought, *and why did it have to keep coming? Did God have no mercy? Had it snowed but six inches less, they would be able to get through, but it had kept snowing, and now they were stuck. That was no one's fault but God's,* she thought. *Only he controls the weather.*

Then she thought to herself, *what if Jack was right? What if that Indian medicine woman had put some kind of curse on them? On her?* She didn't believe in such non-sense, but then again, if Jesus

92

could do miracles, maybe the devil could do the opposite?

Her parents had taught her that God worked for the good of all those who loved him, but that didn't seem to be the case right now. She loved God and she still got sick, and now she was stuck in the snow far from home facing the prospect of freezing to death in the night. Her friend was behind her, moaning, sweating from fever, lying on the hard planks of a wagon bed in a snowstorm. This was not how winter was supposed to be. It was supposed to be snowball fights and sliding down hills, Christmas preparations and good smells from mom's oven, carols and horse-drawn sleighs. Instead, winter had become a terror: horribly cold, long days with no rest, and fitful nights full of bad dreams of a white-faced medicine woman and her angry stare, shouting words she didn't know the meaning of.

Betsy's thoughts had turned very dark, but before they grew darker she did a very smart thing.

Wait, she said to herself.

What would her dad say about all this?

She imagined him home, bed-stricken, coughing and fighting the fever just like Jack was behind her in the wagon. Why did her dad allow her to come on such a long journey in a snowstorm? Certainly he knew it would be dangerous.

Because people needed help, that's why, she thought. Her father believed that God would look after his daughter.

No, that wasn't the right word. It was more than belief. It was trust. Deep trust, for Betsy knew that she was more precious to her father than anything in the world. Her father trusted God even when it came to sending his beloved daughter into the unknown.

She remembered her father singing that hymn before they left. *How did it go?* She sat trying to remember for a moment, and then it came to her:

Fear not, I am with thee; oh, be not dismayed,
for I am thy God and will still give thee aid.
I'll strengthen thee, help thee, and cause thee to stand,
upheld by my righteous omnipotent hand.

Then, quite out of the blue, another thought popped into her head. An idea - from something she'd thought just a moment before.

Jack's father was still tromping through the snow around the wagon, trying to work out what to do next.

"Mr. Fairlane, I have an idea."

CHAPTER 12

A Small Hole in the Clouds

§

"What we really need is a sleigh," said Betsy to Mr. Fairlane.

"Yes, but that's not an idea, that's wishful thinking," he replied.

"But you're a carpenter, and Pete's got some tools under the bench here," she said, standing up and lifting the sitting boards.

"I can't fashion a sleigh out of thin air with a couple hand tools, Betsy," he said.

"What if you pull off the wheels and the axles somehow and let the wagon bed ride right on the snow?"

Jack Sr. thought about this for a moment. He bent over and brushed the snow out from under the wagon so he could get a look at the boards.

"Won't work, there are some cross bars here holding everything together. This thing ain't gonna slide for nothin'."

"But we've got a hammer, a crow bar, a saw, let's see what else," said Betsy, leaning down to search the tool box.

"Hmmm," thought Jack Sr. out loud, "I suppose I could pull some planks off the sides here, salvage the nails, and fix 'em long ways down under here as runners. Ya know Betsy, I think you might be onto something here."

Jack Sr. hopped up and began grabbing tools. He had a quick conversation with Pete as he rifled through the storage box telling him what he was about to do, and Pete approved, which under the circumstances was a no brainer. Jack Sr. laid out the tools at his disposal and started with the crowbar, pulling off boards and planks he planned to use underneath the wagon to convert it to a flat-bottomed sleigh. When he had we he needed, Betsy helped him jack up one side of the wagon by getting the horses to pull it forward as he wedged a brace under the bed. It took some effort to pound the fittings off the wheels to remove them and even more effort to disassemble one side of the front and rear axles. Once the running gear was off, he began fitting long boards lengthwise along the bed, hammering them in with the hardware he'd manage to salvage. Jack Jr. was asleep on the very boards he was pounding into, and Betsy heard him groaning with all the banging that was going on underneath. She wondered what kind of nightmare he was having with all the ruckus going on below him.

When Jack Sr. was content with his handi-work on the right side of the wagon, Betsy had the horses pull the wagon off its brace and it jolted down onto the snow, eliciting more groans from Jack Jr. They both stood a moment inspecting the fruit of the last hour's labor.

"I reckon it'll work," said Jack Sr. to Betsy. "Now we just gotta do the other side. Should go quicker now that we know what we're doing."

They repeated the job on the left side of the wagon and held their breath as Sid and General pulled it off the brace. It was time to see if they'd soon be sleighing their way home or if they'd just turned Pete's wagon into a worthless snow anchor. It wouldn't be easy to undo what they'd just done, so if it didn't work they'd probably have to abandon the wagon altogether.

Betsy climbed into the driver's seat and, after getting a nod from Jack Sr., slapped the reins and clicked her tongue to signal the horses to move out. The wagon sleigh jerked a bit as it slid out of the tamped down snow where'd they'd been working. They'd only gone a few feet before they both realized they had a big problem. The snow was piling up in front of Betsy's feet. It wasn't going to work. Betsy yelled "Ho!" to bring the horses to a stop and Jack Sr. inspected the situation.

"I'm gonna need to ramp the front side of this thing like a skiff so she doesn't plow so much," he said.

"And we ought to move all the weight to the back, too," suggested Betsy.

It took another hour of repurposing boards and hammering them in place. When the new ramped front end was ready, Betsy took to the bench and they tried again. This time it worked. Betsy and Jack Sr. would have jumped for joy if they had the energy, but as it was they just smiled at each other.

Jack Sr. climbed into the back of the wagon bed where his sleeping son lay along with Pete, who was not looking so good. The new design, with the proper weight distribution, slid along on top of the snow without building up a pile in front. Sid and General had no

97

problem pulling it, and finally they got underway again.

The only problem now was that it had taken the full afternoon, and it was starting to get dark. The skies were still spitting snow from thick, grey clouds. Pete did not have a lantern in the wagon, he never travelled at night, and there would be no moon or stars to guide their way. Betsy, who was no stranger to the night, knew it would be too dark to navigate, even with all the snow and their trail still faintly visible. In an hour, they wouldn't be able to see a hand in front of their face. She silently prayed that the clouds would clear out so they could keep going. Her one goal was to get home and the sooner the better. She was exhausted, bleary eyed and still weak from her recovery from the fever, but she didn't want to spend another night in the cold. Her family, her friends, the miners all needed them to deliver the medicine.

After a quick discussion, Jack Sr. and Besty decided to go as far as they could. Thankfully their progress was faster than it had been all trip. The horses instinctively knew to follow the furrow in the snow, and their strong legs were long enough to manage it. Perhaps the horses, too, wanted to get home, back to the comfort of Pete's stable.

By the time they lost the light they'd managed to get through the large meadow and back to the narrow road that ran along the gully towards Goodyear's Bar. Sid's condition had given him good eyesight at night since his pupils had been dilated and let in extra light, but now his eyesight was back to normal along with his night vision.

"I don't know about this," came Jack Sr's voice from the back of the wagon. He was standing as they were moving, trying to see the way ahead. Betsy could make out rock formations on her left and had some sense of the drop to her right, but she was mostly relying on the horses.

"You think we ought to stop here?" asked Betsy.

"You reckon those horses can see better than we can?" asked Jack Sr.

"Well, they're still goin'," said Betsy nervously.

If they went off the side of the road to the right, they could be in big trouble. The gully dropped at least ten, maybe twenty feet from her memory. At some places it was even deeper.

Then something wonderful happened. She looked up and saw a little silver hole in the clouds. It was just enough to cast a sheen of light on the snow. Just enough to see the trail! And the horses kept going. Betsy and Jack Sr. marveled in silence. She thanked God - He'd heard her prayer. The break in the clouds sometimes grew, and then Betsy could see stars, and sometimes shrank until it was just a dim spot, but it remained above them, giving just enough light to guide their way.

When Betsy and Jack Sr. would later tell the story of this trip, their memories would go rather hazy about the next hours. Pete and Jack Jr. were asleep, and Betsy and Jack Sr. must have been close to it. Huddled in their blankets to ward off the cold of the night, they must have drifted in and out of consciousness. Betsy could remember stopping the horses at least once and spreading more feed on the ground, but should could not recall where or when. She thought she could remember passing through a town with all its lights out, but it seemed to her almost like a dream. Jack Sr. admitted to falling asleep, he could account for nothing. They were all weary and terribly exhausted, all fighting off sickness or recovering from it, all drained of emotion after what they'd been through over the past three days.

And then Betsy opened her eyes and realized they weren't moving any more. In the dim, silver light from the little break in the clouds she could see the horses standing still, little puffs of steam curling from their nostrils. They were beside a building which she recognized just a moment later. They were outside of Pete Skagg's stable. General and Sid had somehow led them all the way home.

Besty attempted to stand, but her muscles and joints had become stiff. She struggled to climb over the bench into the back where she shook Pete and Jack Sr.

"Mr. Skaggs, Mr. Fairlane, we're back," she said quietly. The men stirred and opened their eyes.

"By golly, you've brought us all the way home," said Jack Sr.

"Not me, sir, but the horses. They knew the way," responded Betsy.

"How long have I been out?" asked Pete, his voice weak.

"All night. I couldn't tell you what time it is though," replied Betsy.

"Must be nearly dawn," said Jack Sr.

The men fought their own stiff muscles and climbed out of the wagon slowly and clumsily. Jack Sr. lifted Jack Jr. out and held him in his arms like a sleeping baby.

"I'll take Junior home, and I'll be back at sun up for the medicine," said Jack Sr. "I'll be around your place first, Betsy, to see to your dad. You best take some yourself, Pete, before you lie down. I'll fetch it from Mrs. Skaggs in the morning. I'll be needin' a horse if I'm gonna take it up to the camp."

"These horses need a long rest. Take Top Hat," said Pete, who stared longingly at his front door and the warm bed that awaited him just inside.

"Alright. Betsy, you good getting home on your own tonight?"

"Sure, Mr. Fairlane," she replied. Her house wasn't far from the junction where Jack Sr. would turn for home.

The party disbanded quietly with no celebrations for their safe arrival after what had been a horrendous journey. Betsy walked home, found the front door locked, and decided not to knock. She slipped around to the side of the house, jimmied up her window, and crawled into her bedroom. Never had she wanted to escape the outside and get inside so much as she had that night, and she was soon sound asleep.

"Besty?! Betsy!" came her mother's joyful cries the next morning. It was nine o'clock when her mother burst into her room. She sat on the bed, leant over and engulfed her daughter in her arms. Betsy opened her eyes and tried to remember where she was and how she'd got there.

"Mr. Fairlane is at the door, he's come to drop off the medicine," said her mother. "We didn't even know you were back, child! Oh, I am so glad to see you! How did you get in?"

"The window," said Betsy groggily.

"Mr. Fairlane says he needs to talk to you. He's not sure how to prepare the medicine, and he said you knew. He's headed up to the mining camp. He said the medicine had cured you! Poor thing, what an ordeal you've been through! Thank God you're okay!"

Her mother was pouring over here, her eyes damp with tears. Betsy finally gained her senses and sat up, remembering that though they had made it back, their mission was not yet done. Their mission was to get the medicine up to Dr. Marten. She got out of bed, still dressed in her clothes from the night before, and followed her mother out into the front room where Mr. Fairlane was standing by the door with his coat on and his hat in his hands.

She suddenly remember about her pa. "How's dad?" she asked her mother.

She saw a flash of worry cross her mother's face, but her answer was composed and guarded. "He's laid up in bed, but I'm sure he'll be fine, especially now you've got the medicine."

Jack Sr. laid the satchel of tea leaves on the table.

"Well, this is rather odd medicine," said her mother with a confused look on her face. "This is what Doctor Marten told you to get?"

"It's Chinese, mom," said Betsy. "We boil these bits of root to extract the medicine and make tea - simple."

Her mother looked doubtful as she went to put the kettle on the stove to boil some water.

"I've had two cups," called Betsy, "The taste is kinda strong and

102

not altogether pleasant, but I've felt much better ever since. In fact, I want to go up to the camp with Mr. Fairlane to help." The last sentence came out of her mouth before she'd even had the chance to think about it. She realized then that she wanted to complete the mission and to see the fruits of all her troubles of the last few days administered to the men.

"Oh no, my dear, you need to rest," said her mother as she came back from the kitchen.

"But mom, I'm the only one who's already had the fever, which means I'm not likely to get it again. Mr. Fairlane here hasn't had it yet, and if he goes up into that camp, he's likely to get it, and Dr. Marten's going to need help. Why he's probably down with it by now, too, who knows what we'll find when we get up there. It might be more than one man can handle, and I make a very good nurse," said Betsy, now talking very quickly.

"Betsy, your father and I have been praying for you for the last three days worried sick. Your father was troubled, he thought he'd made a grave mistake in sending you, and to be honest, I never would have approved of it if he'd asked me. It's been no small matter between us over the last three days."

"But mom, the reason he sent me *then* is the same reason I should go *now* – because people need help," urged Betsy. "And we're Christians, we're supposed to sacrifice ourselves to help others. I'm not going to hide out in my little warm parsonage while people freeze to death or die of sickness like some lousy…no-man-of-God!"

"What on earth are you talking about?" asked her mother.

Besty sighed. "The pastor down in Nevada City wouldn't help us, mom. He wouldn't let us sleep in his church overnight to get out of the cold. It was unbelievable! He couldn't be bothered to go out of his way one inch! I don't ever want to be like him. Can you please go ask dad if I can go?"

Her mother stood staring at her daughter. She, too, was once just like Betsy. Her father was also a preacher called to a wild place - South Africa, and she'd wanted to be just like him. He was brave and ambitious for the Lord's work. It was her father who'd inspired her and Henry to venture into the American frontier to pastor a church. There'd been moments of danger, and they'd fully expected them, but they'd not been dissuaded and carried on with courage and tenacity. Now her daughter was following in their footsteps. *No*, she corrected herself, *in Jesus' footsteps*. It was him that had set the example they'd followed. He was the reason for their bravery. It was his selflessness and passion that guided them, and now, her daughter wanted to follow those same footsteps.

Betsy saw the expression on her mother's face change as she stood there thinking.

"Mr. Fairlane, Henry and I are greatly indebted to you for bringing our daughter home. Please do so again, by this evening if you can," she said with a smile.

"Yes ma'am," said Jack Sr.

Betsy gave her mom a huge hug.

CHAPTER 13

HANK'S BLUFF

§

Mr. Fairlane agreed to ride back to Mr. Skaggs stable and saddle up Sally Sue for Betsy while she changed her clothes and had some breakfast. Having skipped two meals the day before, she was rightly starving, and her mother fried twice as many eggs as normal and buttered three slices of bread. Betsy devoured them quickly while the tea brewed, and then, when the tea was ready, they went in to see her father.

Betsy had never seen him so gaunt and colorless. He looked worse than her mother had let on. Nonetheless, he smiled when he opened his eyes and saw his daughter. She sat on the side of the bed and held his hand. She softly reassured him that she was alright and avoided recounting how harrowing her adventure had actually been. She explained how she'd already had the fever and how the Bai Hu Tang tea they'd bought from Mr. Bao had cured it. Betsy expected he'd recover just like she'd had, and her hopeful optimism brightened his mood.

She didn't say she was heading up to the miner's camp, but only gave him a kiss on the cheek before she left him to rest. Back in the front room she donned her coat, hat, and mittens and hugged her mother goodbye. Her mother kissed her and out she went, back into the cold, hopping down the steps between the heaps of snow piled around their front walk and to the road where she ran towards Pete's house.

Mr. Fairlane had Sally Sue saddled by the time she got there. As she came in she looked into Sid's stall and saw him asleep on the ground. If you didn't know, horses have an uncanny ability to sleep standing up, a trait they'd developed over the ages for their own defense, but Sid was so exhausted that he'd lied down for a proper rest. He'd certainly earned it.

"You ready to go?" asked Mr. Fairlane.

"Yes sir," replied Betsy.

At the sound of her voice, Sid's ears perked up. He opened his eyes and lifted his head. Betsy peaked through the stable door, and then, almost as if he'd been embarrassed to be caught lying down, he pushed his legs out and went about the rather awkward contortions of getting to his feet.

Once he was up, Betsy patted him on the neck and said, "You did it again, boy. You looked after us and got us home. I don't know how you did it, but you did. You're an amazing animal, you know that?"

Sid lapped up the attention from his favorite human.

"But today, you need to rest," she said. She kissed him on the muzzle and walked down to take the reins of Sally Sue. As they walked out of the stable, Sid jerked his head and whinnied. He seemed to be jealous of Sally Sue, perhaps even offended that Betsy would go out on another horse. Or maybe he also wanted to complete the mission.

Betsy paused by his stable with Sally Sue just behind. "You can stay home today," she called back to Sid.

Sid seemed to understand what she'd said, and suddenly he reared back, keeping his head low as not to hit it on a rafter, and banged his front hooves down right onto the top beam of the partition wall. Besty jumped back, and even Mr. Fairlane was caught off-guard. Sid stood there like that, front hooves resting on the beam, in protest.

"Well, seems the tables have turned," said Jack Sr. with a chuckle. "I think he wants to go."

Just like Betsy, who'd just minutes ago had convinced her mother to let her go, Sid was now employing the same tactics on Betsy.

"What do you think?" asked Besty to Jack Sr.

"I think it'd be alright. He's had a rest and some feed, same as you," he laughed. "And he's just as stubborn, too."

It only took a few minutes to unsaddle Sally Sue and saddle Sid, and soon they were off. Betsy marveled as Sid came out of the dim stables into the brightness of winter without batting an eye. He was cured, and she was happy. They were both happy. It felt like all the troubles of the last three days were a distant memory and this was a new day.

"You know the way?" asked Jack Sr.

"I do," said Betsy confidently, then she kicked her heels and yelled "Yah!" Sid surged forward into a gallop instantly, as if he'd been waiting to stretch his legs like this since the day he'd gone blind. There was no hint of fatigue despite the miles he'd covered the day before and through the night pulling a sleigh laden with four people. The snow parted before him, exploding in chunks as his hooves pounded through. At Jack Sr.'s command, Tophat followed, and that is how the pair of horses and riders went, all the way through town, a vapor of white mist hanging in their wake. Children heard the muffled sound of hooves and ran to the windows to see the sight, Sid, the magnificent black steed, piloted by a young girl, her coat flying up behind from the speed at which they were travelling. On they went without slowing, out of town, up past the mill, over the creek, and on up the long climb to Hank's Bluff. In twenty minutes the camp was in sight.

The canvas tents of the mining camp sagged under a heavy layer of snow. Smoke rose in two columns, one from a campfire tended by a man hunched next to it, another from the mess tent with a wood burner inside. It was very quiet for a mining camp. The man looked up from the fire as they approached and rose to his feet. Betsy recognized him, a short Irishman called Clancy. He'd been one of the thieves in the attempted gold heist, but since then he'd changed his ways, or so it seemed from his occasional presence in her father's church on Sundays. He gave them a friendly wave and walked over to where Betsy and Jack Sr. were tying up the horses.

"Howdy friends," he said with a slight accent. "What brings you up this way?"

"We have the medicine the doctor ordered," said Jack Sr.

Clancy looked at Betsy inquisitively. He recognized her from church, but it was certainly unusual to see a young girl outside of town, let alone in camp. Little did he know that if it weren't for Betsy's plan after the attempted gold heist, they never would have found gold in Hank's Bluff.

"She's my nurse," said Jack. Clancy nodded.

"He's in the mess tent, but I best take it in. Everyone's got the fever," said Clancy.

"I've already had it, so I can go in and help the doctor administer the medicine to the men," said Betsy boldly.

"I see, well let's go then," said Clancy. "I've had it, too. Seems I got off easy, some of the men are in rough shape," he said as they made their way to the mess tent. Jack Sr. stayed with the horses. Clancy went on, "We done moved cots for the worst into the mess tent where it's warm, but some are still in their own tents. Injin' Joe done disappeared for a while, went back to his tribe, but they wouldn't let him stay. Kicked 'im out they did, and now he's back here. Them injin's know better I guess."

Clancy pulled back the flap of the mess tent for Betsy and she went in. The scene inside was unnerving. Eight cots were packed tightly, each with a man in some state of distress or asleep. The smell made her want to wretch, though that was not so uncommon for miners. Dr. Marten sat in a chair with his head in his hands. When he noticed Betsy come in he rose wearily, looking frail and colorless, no doubt fighting the disease himself.

"This here's the nurse," said Clancy, then he looked over and whispered, "what's your name again?"

"Besty," she whispered back.

"Nurse Betsy. She's already had the fever, so she's come to help give the medicine."

Dr. Marten blinked. He hadn't expected a nurse, but it was welcome news.

"Clancy, can you fill that kettle there with enough water for tea for everyone? That's how we'll administer the medicine. Gather the cups too, give them a good wash and bring them in," said Betsy confidently.

Clancy stared for a moment, surprised she knew his name and surprised further to be given orders. But he followed her instructions without complaint and set upon his tasks.

"Did you get the sulphorous acid?" asked the Doctor.

"No, Mr. Bao gave us something else. Something Chinese," she said in a whisper. "I took it and it cured me, but it tastes a bit like...grass."

"Doesn't matter, as long as it works. We're in desperate need here."

Betsy got out the satchel of Bai Hu Tang and showed the doctor. Clancy brought the kettle and they got to work, the three of them going from bed to bed handing out cups of bitter, steaming Chinese tea.

When they were through in the mess tent, Clancy and Betsy went outside from tent to tent, giving the medicine to the rest of the men.

They still had a fair amount of dried leaves in the little sack thanks to Pete for going back for more when they were leaving Nevada City.

"What is this stuff anyway," asked Clancy when they were through. "I ain't ever seen no medicine like that before, apart from the Chamomile my mammy used to drink before bed."

"A special remedy. A thousand years old, or so the druggist said," replied Besty. She didn't mention he was Chinese.

"You sure are young for a nurse," mused Clancy.

"Oh, I'm not a nurse, I just wanted to help."

"I seen you in church, I didn't think you was a nurse."

"Jesus taught us to love our neighbor, that's why I'm here."

"We're hardly neighbors," laughed Clancy.

"But you are," replied Betsy. "Don't you remember the story of the good Samaritan? Everyone is our neighbor, even strangers."

"You're the preacher's kid, ain't ya?" observed Clancy.

"Yes, Reverend Wescott is my father."

"Well he brought you up right, I reckon. Only thing my pappy ever taught me was how to drink and swear."

Betsy remembered Clancy letting loose a string a insults at her from the bottom of a mine shaft, which coincidently, lay just over the ridge from where they were at that moment. She still remembered some of those taunts, they were burned into her memories of that crazy night. But oddly, she now felt a sudden compassion for the little Irishman. Perhaps he'd never known anything but a father who'd sworn and drank in all his life. Perhaps he'd never known the kindness and love of a caring parent.

111

"Well, I should hope I'll never hear a swear from you," Betsy told him. "It just wouldn't be right to call a girl a mud-eating pig-dog now would it?"

Clancy cocked his head at her in a funny way. "No ma'am, although that does sound like something I'd say..." his voice trailed off.

It was, in fact, something he'd said, though the butt-end of a falling pistol had erased it from his mind.

Mr. Fairlane walked up and asked, "Have you seen everyone now?"

"I believe so, yessir," said Clancy.

"Good," replied Jack Sr. "I checked in with the doctor and got a list of things he needs. I can run them up here tomorrow. I reckon our job here's done."

Jack and Betsy said goodbye to Clancy, climbed onto their horses and turned towards Downieville. It wasn't even noon yet. The last part of their mission had been the easiest. They let the horses walk slowly down the hill from Hank's Bluff. They crossed over the creek at the bottom and were soon on the road that went south into Downieville. It was silent and peaceful, and Betsy had a warm feeling of accomplishment - their mission was finally complete.

She felt safe with Mr. Fairlane and his rifle beside her, and with Sid, her protector, below her. She could admire the snow again knowing that soon she'd be back in the comfort and warmth of her own home. In fact, she felt better than she had for three days. She was still a little achy from the long journey and the fever, but the worst was behind her. Of course, there were many others who were sick, and quite seriously from what she'd just seen, but now that they'd had Bao's medicine, she was sure they'd all recover. After all, if she'd recovered, so could they. Just a day ago it seemed that everything that could go wrong had gone wrong: the snowstorm, scarlet fever, the wagon getting stuck, then stuck again... Now it seemed, for the moment at least, that everything would be alright.

That moment lasted about three minutes, then it suddenly disappeared. A piercing yell came down from the ridge above them. A familiar, terrible yell.

Betsy and Jack Sr. looked up, startled, and Jack instantly grabbed for his rifle. There, standing above them about a hundred feet away, was a bear, its muzzle painted red, and an old woman riding on its back with the lower half of her face painted bone-chilling white. She was screaming something in her native tongue and holding something out at arm's length that looked like a dead animal.

Betsy's nightmares were suddenly alive once again, but this time they were all too real.

CHAPTER 14

CURSE OF THE BEAR WITCH

§

Mr. Fairlane gripped his rifle. He did not raise it, but kept it in plain sight on his lap. They stood stationary in the road, Sid and Top Hat shifting uneasily below them. The horses kept their eyes on the bear with the human on its back and pawed the ground with their hooves, showing they were ready to run.

The story Jack Sr. had heard from his son hadn't quite prepared him for what he was seeing with his own two eyes. The bear was huge and surly looking. It appeared aged, but no less dangerous for its years. The bear's fur around its face was painted like the woman's, except red around the muzzle. If war paint was meant to inspire fear, it was doing a good job. The woman herself was not so much frightening as haunting, her white-painted face like that of a ghost, her eyes glaring angrily, her voice shouting her strange native language. Jack Sr. was not a man easily alarmed, but his heart was beating like a drum.

At the sight of her nightmare's return Betsy could have locked up like she did before, but she didn't. Perhaps her nightmares had helped, for the sight was less shocking than it had been the first time.

That didn't stop Betsy's stomach from convulsing into a tight ball. She almost felt as though she were going to throw up. She was clenching the reins so tightly her fingers had gone white.

"What do we do?" she asked.

"Just stay calm. Let's keep going, but slowly. Stay behind me. If she starts coming down the hill, my rifle is going to come up. You and Sid bolt."

Jack Sr. urged Top Hat forward slowly and Betsy fell in behind and to the left, putting them between her and the bear. She wondered if Sid could feel her knees shaking. She didn't take her eyes off the woman. She couldn't make out any of the words she was saying, they were all ones she hadn't heard before. What she held out at arm's length wasn't a dead animal as they'd first thought. It was some kind of garment, dull gray in color, and she held it and waved it as if it had some kind of significance, though why Betsy had no idea. Then the old woman threw it down in the snow and spat on it. It startled Betsy, and Jack Sr. looked back at her to make sure she was alright.

Thankfully, the woman and bear showed no signs of descending the ridge down to the road where Jack Sr. and Betsy were. She only continued to yell words in her native tongue. That she was angry was unquestionable, but Betsy did not hear the same phrases she'd heard before.

"Just keep going forward, we're almost by," said Jack Sr. Betsy kept silent.

When they'd gone far enough that it became awkward to strain their necks to see her, the medicine woman stopped her yelling. When they looked back a few moments later, she was gone.

"Well, guess I've met the Bear Witch," said Jack Sr. "She ain't the friendliest of Indians. Not that I've met many that are. Though she didn't seem to care much for us, either, I suppose."

Betsy didn't yet have the words to reply. After a few more minutes, Jack Sr. put his rifle back in the saddle, having judged they were safe.

"You alright over there?" he asked. He knew she'd been quite affected by her first encounter with the medicine woman. It had taken a second disaster, their trip to Nevada City, to make her forget her first.

"Yes sir. Let's just get back to Downieville," she replied.

Jack Sr. pushed Top Hat up to a trot and Betsy and Sid followed. They didn't say anything on the way back, and in a half hour they were back at Pete's place.

As they unsaddled the horses, Jack Sr. said, "Don't you mind about that old squaw, if she meant to do us any harm she would of. I reckon she's just mad at us white folk for movin' into their territory. It ain't like there isn't enough land for everyone, but them Indians don't see it that way. They ain't pleased with us settlers, and that's why we got so much trouble."

Betsy listened but said nothing.

"She probably comes from that the little Indian village up at Rattlesnake Diggins," Jack went on. "It ain't far from Hank's Bluff, just north and west a ways. There can't be more than twenty Indians there, and they'll probably be movin' on soon since we've crossed paths with them, assuming she's one of 'em. I can assure you, it ain't nothing to worry about."

"Thank you, Mr. Fairlane," said Betsy as she hung the final piece of tack on a hook in the stable and made sure Sid had feed and water. "I'm glad to have joined you to administer the medicine up at the mining camp. Our mission's finally done. Now we can only hope and pray everyone recovers. Please give my regards to Jack, and have him stop by as soon as he's well enough. If you don't mind, I might stop in on him later to see how he's doing."

"Of course, Betsy," Jack Sr. said with smile. He was relieved she was taking this encounter better than the last, at least as far as he could tell.

Betsy walked home through the snow, her feet starting to go cold, though not as cold as the last few days on the trail. But she wasn't thinking about her feet, she was thinking about those painted faces, one belonging to a woman, the other belonging to a bear. Last night she hadn't had nightmares about them. Now those nightmares would be back.

Her mother was relieved when the door opened and her daughter came into the front room. She rushed over and hugged her.

"Well, that didn't take long! Thank the Lord you're back safe! How did it go?" she asked, helping Betsy with her coat.

"We saw the Bear Witch again," she said. Her mother froze and stared at her in disbelief. "She found us coming back from Hank's Bluff. She was angry, ma, I don't know why, but she just yelled and yelled."

"Did she do anything? Was the bear with her?" her mother asked, still in shock.

"Yes, she was on the bear, but they just stood above us on this ridge and yelled. She threw a piece of cloth down on the ground and spat on it."

Her mother gathered her into her arms. "Now there, don't you worry about her. I'll bet Mr. Fairlane is already on his way to see the Sheriff. We'll let the men handle it, and I'm sure it'll be just fine. You can stay tucked up here in our safe little home and you haven't got a thing to worry about."

The adults sure had a lot of useless comforting words, thought Betsy sullenly.

"Well, did you get the medicine to the miners?" asked her mother, eager to change the subject.

"Yes, I saw to each and every one. That little Irishman from church helped me, Clancy. Dr. Marten looked quite ill himself, and Mr. Fairlane stayed back so as not to catch it. I just wish I felt better about it, but the only thing I can think about is that angry old woman."

"Well, I am proud of you for going up there today. Your Grandad would have been especially proud. That was a very brave thing you did, and a very merciful one as well. I think the Lord is pleased with his servant today," her mother said, squeezing her affectionately.

"If he's pleased, he's sure got a funny way of showing it," said Betsy.

"Well, he works in mysterious ways," said her mother. "I can't pretend to understand either, but maybe one day we will."

"Is dad feeling any better?" asked Betsy.

"Not yet, dear, but he will be. Give it time."

"Can I go see him?"

"He's resting, but I'll let you take him some soup when he wakes."

"I brought some medicine back with me so we can make some more tea," said Betsy.

"That's the spirit," said her mother, smiling.

The afternoon passed slowly. She was dreading the coming night when she'd have to sleep. She knew what was coming once she closed her eyes. She wished Molly could come over, but with her Dad ill their house was off limits for any visitors. They were in quarantine. All she could do was try to distract herself.

She sat in the front room with a blanket around her and picked up the latest Harper's Weekly from the side table. It probably wasn't the latest, just the latest to have made its way all the way up to Downieville. There was a drawing of a family decorating a pine tree on the front cover. Christmas trees were at that time a new thing and not yet a tradition as they are now. Besty had never seen one in real life, but the picture made it look charming and lovely, and she wondered if her parents would let her go up and cut down a sapling to decorate like the one on the magazine. Bringing a tree inside seemed a bit silly, they hardly had space as it was, but all the children were so happy in the picture, playing on the floor around the tree without a care in the world, and that's what she wanted at the moment - to be free from worry. Free of anxiety. Free of fear.

That night she lay in bed and the visions of the Bear Witch came flooding into her mind. The face paint, the angry glare, all of it. It was all just as her nightmares had been, all except for one thing. What was the grey cloth? How did that fit in?

Suddenly she sat straight up in bed. It hit her. That was her cloth - her blanket! The one she'd dropped on the way to Nevada City as a gift to the Indian boy! Of course!

And then a further realization came upon her, one she did not welcome at all, one so terrible that it made her throat go tight. *She'd seen that boy just before she'd become ill.* She'd used that small blanket as a scarf, over her mouth. It must have been covered in scarlet fever. She brought her hands to her face as tears began to well up in her eyes. *Had she spread scarlet fever to an Indian village? Is that why the woman was so angry?* It had to be. It all made sense. That's why she'd thrown the blanket down and spat on it. Betsy was responsible for spreading disease to the Indians.

In her dreams that night she saw the old Indian woman's white face floating above the red jaws of the bear. Saliva dripped as it looked hungrily at her. Huge claws scraped against the ground. The old woman held in her hand the blanket, Betsy's gift to the boy - the gift of disease. Her eyes glowed like a demon's, her mouth yawned open like a ghost, and out of it came wretched words, seething with hate, only this time she could understand them:

"You brought sickness and death to my people! Evil girl! The spirits will punish you! First white people come and take our land, then you take the lives of our children! Leave us alone! Go away, or I will curse you! Take your disease and your greed for gold and your guns and leave, or I will curse you!"

Betsy tossed and turned, beads of sweat on her forehead as she fought away the bear and the woman in her dreams. She clutched the blanket on her bed with white knuckles, and then suddenly found herself sitting up, fear still hanging in the dark room.

It was only a dream, she told herself. *Only another dream.*

She laid back down, but images of the ghostly woman would not leave her mind. She kept her eyes open and forced herself to think good thoughts - summertime down at the river, jumping off rocks into the cool water, climbing trees and running down sandy hillsides, and sunset rides with Molly and Jack on Pete's horses. But every time she closed her eyes, the fear returned. There was only one thing to do now. She got out of bed, left her bedroom, and found her mother.

The front room was dimly lit by the silvery light of the snow outside reflected through the windows. She could see her mother asleep on a made up bed on the living room floor. She'd not slept in the bedroom with her father since he'd fallen ill.

Betsy went over, knelt beside her, and said softly, "Mother, are you awake?"

She stirred and propped herself up on an elbow. "What is it Betsy?"

"I had a nightmare. I keep having them. And I think I need to tell you something. It's…important," said Betsy quietly.

"Well, okay," she said wearily. She slowly rose to her feet and lit a candle on the little end table near her. "Let me put the kettle on and we can talk."

Mary Wescott went into the kitchen to boil the kettle for tea. Her mother's instinct told her this was important, and hot tea would both wake her up and soothe whatever conversation was about to occur. She returned to front room while the kettle boiled and they both sat in the light of the candle.

"So, tell me about this dream," she said.

All of Betsy's anxiety spilled out in words as she told her mother about the nightmares.

"But there's something more," Betsy said. "There's something I didn't tell you about what happened today. The medicine woman had with her a blanket that I dropped off of the wagon on our way to Nevada City. I saw an Indian boy up in the hills watching us as we went, I think we were around Goodyear's Bar, not far into the journey yet, and he looked cold, so I let the blanket I had been wearing as a scarf to keep my face warm fall to the ground. It was snowing hard and it was bitterly cold, but I thought I could spare it for his sake, he was only young and seemed all alone. I didn't know if he was lost or abandoned or what, but anyway, after that I started to feel sick, and, well, I think that Indian boy picked up that blanket, took it back to his village, and now the fever has spread there as well. I gave them the disease, and somehow that medicine woman figured all this out, that's why she was so angry. She threw the blanket down and spit on it."

Her mother stared in astonishment for a moment. This certainly was not what she'd expected to hear. "Now, let's take this slowly. First of all, there is no way you could have known that your blanket would infect them, you were feeling fine at the time, so you certainly can't blame yourself for this. And we're not even sure that's what's happened. The medicine woman was angry the first time you saw her, so there's no reason to think that disease is what's caused her to be angry again. She might be angry at all white folk, not just you. The blanket, if it's the same one you dropped, might be just her saying that she doesn't want white people's gifts because she doesn't like white people."

"It was the same blanket mom, I know it," said Betsy. "That boy is probably sick, maybe even dying. And I'm sure he told her where he got it and who he got it from. Clancy said that one of the miners is an Indian and he tried to go back home when he got sick, but they wouldn't let him back. So they know the miners have got the disease. Maybe she's even been watching the camp. She's worked it all out, don't you see? And it's all my fault!"

"But Betsy, you couldn't have known!"

"That doesn't change the fact that it's my fault," she replied.

"Betsy, diseases spread, that's what they do. The miners picked it up from somewhere and they gave it to Mr. Barley, and Mr. Barley unknowingly gave it to your father and you. It's the nature of all sicknesses, and it's outside our control. So you must put away these thoughts that you're somehow to blame."

"I suppose," said Betsy. They could hear the kettle boiling and her mother got up to take it off the stove. Betsy followed her into the kitchen and sat at the table. "Oh mother, what else could go wrong? Everything has been a disaster since we ran into that woman...the storm, the sickness, the trip to Nevada City. Dad's got it, Jack's got it, Pete's got it, the doctor's even got it. Now the Indian village has got it, and probably the whole town is next."

"It's a good thing you went to get that medicine then," said her mother consolingly.

"Good for us, but that doesn't help the poor Indians," replied Betsy.

"They've probably got their own medicine," suggested her mother.

"Well if their medicine is as a good as their medicine woman, then I don't think they have much hope. You know, sometimes I think she did put a curse on me. That's what Jack thinks you know, and I'm starting to believe it."

"The only curse that woman put on you was the curse of fear," said her mother as she sipped her tea. "And that's what we've got to work out of you. The question is, how are we going to do that?"

CHAPTER 15

A CURE FOR FEAR

§

The late-night conversation with her mother had put her mind enough at ease that she was able to go back to bed and fall asleep. She slept late into the morning, still tired as she was from those long days battling illness and the snowstorm. It was a relief to wake up and not have to go anywhere. She fully intended to stay put, cuddle into a warm blanket, and do pretty much nothing.

Her mother, who served as the town's only school teacher, had cancelled school classes on account of Reverend Wescott's illness. The children were, of course, overjoyed. They spent long hours building snow forts and sledding down the many hills that surrounded Downieville. Betsy, for the first time in her life, was quite happy to let them go on without her.

Her dad was feeling a little better, or so he said, but his forehead was still warm to the touch and his color not right. Betsy fixed him some more of the Chinese tea and tried not to worry. What worried her more was the thought of that Indian boy, stricken with illness, and who knows who else, perhaps their whole village. Maybe it wasn't her fault, she told herself, because she couldn't have known. But then again, maybe it was.

She also remembered what her mother said last night about the curse of fear. She'd never known much of fear in her lifetime, she'd never had much to fear. Yes, that incident with Clancy and Curly and Barley up at Hank's Bluff had been frightening, but at least she'd known her enemy then. She'd known what she was getting into, after all, she'd planned most of it herself, even if it hadn't gone to plan. The Bear Witch was something else entirely, something foreign and strange and not altogether natural. Something she had no control over whatsoever. The old woman's anger was a force of its own. It felt different than greed, which was what had driven those miners to do what they'd done. Greed she could understand. This was worse. This was something worth fearing.

She'd been praying about it, praying the bad thoughts would go away, but it didn't seem to help. She remembered her father's hymn that had helped her keep going in the snow storm. She sang it quietly back to herself:

"Fear not, I am with thee; oh, be not dismayed,
for I am thy God and will still give thee aid.
I'll strengthen thee, help thee, and cause thee to stand,
upheld by my righteous omnipotent hand!"

But the words didn't take away the heavy feeling in her stomach. It probably comforted her mother to hear her singing it more than her, she thought. She longed for something to put her mind at ease. *Perhaps the Bible had some verses that would help,* she thought.

"Hey ma, what are some verses about fear?" she asked. Her mother was sitting in their second comfiest chair knitting repairs in her father's socks.

Her fingers stopped their handiwork and she looked up at the ceiling. "Well let me think for a moment," she replied.

"How about this one: Perfect love casts out fear," she said after a moment.

"Where's that one?" asked Betsy, standing up to get the family Bible off the shelf.

"First John, I believe," said her mother.

Betsy looked up first John and found it in chapter four. She read the verse out loud:

> "There is no fear in love; but perfect love casts out fear, because fear hath torment."

"Well, if by torment he means nightmares, he's got at least that much right," said Betsy.

"Fear can torment you while you're awake, too," her mother said. "I felt tormented when you'd been gone for three days and I didn't know if you were coming back. I feared something terrible had happened."

"So what did you do?" asked Betsy.

"I prayed a lot, and your father and I talked about it a lot, and we

127

provided some comfort for each other."

"Did your fear go away?"

"Not really, but I felt a little better," replied her mother.

"The verse says perfect love casts out fear. What do you suppose that means?" asked Betsy.

"Well, it could mean a couple of things I suppose," said her mother. "Why don't you read more of that chapter to see if you can figure it out for yourself. Sometimes we need a bit of context to understand what the writer is trying to say."

Betsy sat and read the whole of the fourth chapter of first John. She didn't understand the first part about testing false spirits, but the second part about loving one another was familiar. John wrote to urge Christians to love one another because love is from God, and God is love. It even says anyone who doesn't love doesn't know God! *That was pretty strong language*, Besty thought.

She continued reading. It said God showed his love by sending Jesus for our sake, to die for our sins. If God loved us that much, then we ought to love others the same way, and when we do so his love is perfected in us.

There was the key word, Betsy thought. *'Perfected.' It was a clue. Perfect love casts out fear,* she remembered, *and perfect love loves others the way God loves us. Okay, that makes sense,* she thought.

She kept reading. There was more on 'perfect' love. It said whoever lives a life of love, God lives within them, and when God lives within us, we need not fear the day of judgment. Then comes the first verse she read: there is no fear in love, but perfect love casts out fear.

"So maybe," she finally said to her mother, "the fear the verse is referring to is the fear of judgment day. The fear that we will be found guilty for our sins. But love casts out this fear because Jesus died for us and Jesus lives in us when we love."

"That sounds right. What do you mean by love, though? Who's loving who?" asked her mother.

"Well, it talks about all kinds of love - God's love for us, our love for him, our love for others, it's like one big triangle of love between Him and us and everyone else."

"Yes, that sounds like the Kingdom of Heaven alright," nodded her mother. "So let's see if I can apply this to my case. When I was fearing while you were away, I suppose I needed to remember God's love for me and for you, knowing that he would look after us like his own children, which I should know by now. He's been so gracious to me so many times before, and yet I forget."

"And for me and the Bear Witch, I guess I have to love her?" asked Betsy with a measure of doubt in her voice.

"Well, God does say love your enemies, so that's a good starting place. At least we must give them the benefit of the doubt and realize they, too, must have a story we don't know about. But that might not be all…"

"I need to trust God, too, since I'm one of his children?"

"Yes, that too, but I'm thinking of another way we love God. Somewhere else in the Bible it says we abide in his love when we keep his commandments, when we do what he'd want us to do. We need to stop and consider what he would want us to do, and then do it."

"But mom, I've been trying to do the right thing this whole time!" said Betsy.

"And God has looked after you, hasn't he?"

Betsy thought about that for a moment. It had been hard going since she met the Bear Witch, but she'd come through it in the end, and got the medicine as well. Her mother had a point, God *had* looked after her.

"Then why am I still afraid?" Betsy asked.

"I think it's okay if you're afraid. Fear is an emotion God has given you for your own protection, so long as it doesn't stop you from being his servant and loving others."

"Am I not loving others enough?" asked Betsy.

"Love starts in your heart, but always has to come out in your actions, like when you decided to help get that medicine."

"So is there something more I need to do?"

"Maybe," said her mother.

"Well, that's no help."

"I can think of one thing," said her mother.

"What?"

"You're not going to like it," she said.

"Apologize to someone?"

Her mother laughed and said, "No. At least that's not what I was thinking."

"Well, what were you thinking?"

"It sounds like there's an Indian village that could use that medicine."

"What? You mean take the medicine to the Indians?" asked Betsy. Her shock was not at the idea, but that her mother, as protective as she was, had suggested it.

"Yes."

"Me?"

"Us."

"You and me?" asked Betsy. She was so shocked she stood up and looked at her mom with her mouth hanging open.

"I thought about it last night, and of course I didn't like the idea at first," her mother said. "But the more I thought about it, and the more I thought about what God would want, the more I realized that that's what we need to do."

"Why us, why not..." Betsy's voice trailed off as she tried to think of who could take the medicine to the Indians. The doctor was both sick and busy with the miners, Pete was sick, Jack was sick, his dad didn't like Indians, her dad was sick, even the one Indian in the mining camp was sick, and he'd already tried to go back home.

"I thought of that, too, but..." said her mother.

"There's no one else," Besty said, completing her sentence. "Who will look after Dad?"

"I've already discussed it with him. He'll be just fine. He's not completely helpless, he's just got a fever."

Betsy thought about what it would mean to go to the Indian village, and there was one obstacle that loomed largest in her mind.

"Mom, I can't face...her," she said, and then, without Betsy's consent her eyes starting filling with tears.

"You've never met your Grandpa Andrew in South Africa. He's a quiet, unassuming man, but stronger and braver than anyone I know. Do you know what he's doing in South Africa?"

"He's a pastor like dad, isn't he?"

"Yes, but he's also a missionary. He founded the South African General Mission just a little over ten years ago. He was sixty years old then and still had a heart to reach African tribes...their *Indians*. Your dad and I had the same heart when we moved out here. We wanted to take the gospel to the Indians as much as we wanted to take it to our own people. That's how we ended up in this little frontier town."

"But I've never seen you two go out to the Indians," Besty said curiously.

"Well, it proved harder than we thought. And just keeping our little church and school going kind of took all our time. But the desire to reach out to them has never left me. It's always been in the back of my mind. They need to know about Jesus, too."

"But mom, you haven't seen the Bear Witch. You don't want to see the Bear Witch. She doesn't want our medicine and she doesn't want our Gospel, I'm sure of it. If you'd seen what I've seen, you'd know."

"But what about the rest of the village?" her mother asked.

"Mom, if she's there, we won't even get into the village! We probably won't even get near it! She has a *bear*!"

Her mom paused for a moment, but there was no sign of wavering in her expression. Her face was a picture of compassion that would not be shaken.

"Betsy, do you believe perfect love casts out fear?" asked her mother.

"I don't know..." Betsy replied.

"Then let's see if the promise is true. Let's trust Him and do what He'd have us do."

CHAPTER 16

BEST MADE PLANS AND TELEGRAMS

♪

There was a lot to do to prepare for their trip to the Indian village. The first thing was to find out where they were going. Betsy decided to visit Jack to get that information since he'd seen it on his day out with Pete and his dad. She went to his place, and his mother met her at the door. Jack's mother's name was Susan, and she was happy to see Betsy. Jack Jr. was laid up on a sofa in their living room but feeling much better than he had the day before. His fever was mild and the rash was receding, though he claimed it was due to his own good health, not "that wacky Chinese stuff," as he called it.

He'd of course heard all about Betsy's encounter with the Bear Witch from his father, who'd gone off to see the sheriff as soon as he'd returned to insist that a letter be sent to the U.S. Army requesting their aid to relocate the Indians. Betsy was not surprised by this news, but it did rather complicate things. She wasn't sure how she should tell Jack she was planning to visit that very village to take them medicine.

"Jack, there's something I didn't tell your dad," Betsy began. "The Bear Witch had a blanket in her hand. It was from our trip to

Nevada City. It was the one you handed me when we stopped, and I wrapped around my neck. I dropped it on the road, on purpose. There was an Indian boy, and he looked cold, so I left it for him. And then I got sick. The Bear Witch spat on that blanket, and I think I know why. I think their village has scarlet fever as well. That boy caught the fever from me, and she knew it. She figured it out."

"Well you ought not feel bad about that, you didn't even know you were sick at the time," replied Jack.

"What if the whole village has it? They'll be in no better shape than the miners."

"Guess that's their tough luck," said Jack.

"But we have medicine..." suggested Betsy.

"Oh, no," exclaimed Jack. "No, no, no, we're not going to take the medicine to those Indians. No way."

"I'm not asking you to," replied Betsy, trying not to be put off by Jack's opinion, although her body language couldn't hide it.

"Good," he said.

"I just need you to tell me where the village is," requested Betsy.

"Oh come on Betsy, you are not going there alone," said Jack, rolling his eyes.

"No, I'm not. I'm not going alone. I'm going with my ma. It was her idea. So, how do I get there?"

"Betsy, this is not a good idea," Jack tried to persuade her.

Betsy folded her arms and gave him a steely look, a look he'd seen before when she was being stubborn. It meant she wasn't going to budge.

135

"Alright, fine. It ain't hard. Go to where we ran into the Bear Witch, then keep following that same ridge to the north. In a quarter mile or so you'll be able to look down to your left and see the village. There's just a half dozen or so huts down there. They'll be covered in snow of couse, they'll probably just look like a bunch of lumps from the ridge, but no doubt you'll see smoke, unless they've moved on already."

Besty hopped up to her feet and said, "Well, I'm glad you're feeling better. Your father okay?"

"Yeah, somehow he's got off scot-free, he's working on Pete's wagon out back," said Jack in reply. "He's got some idea to improve it, make it convert from wagon to sleigh and back again for these winter snows."

"That sounds clever. I'll let you know how the mission goes," she said as she was leaving.

"As if a curse ain't enough, you're gonna go get yourself killed," grumble Jack as she closed the front door behind her.

Outside Betsy paused on the Fairlane porch, closed her eyes, and took a deep breath. *What on earth was she thinking - walking into the Bear Witch's territory?*

Betsy trudged through the snow to Pete's house, where Pete's wife Shelly let her in.

"How's Mr. Skaggs feeling today?" asked Betsy politely.

"He's resting, still feverish but no worse," she replied. She looked tired and somewhat pale herself. "Can I give him a message from you?"

"Would you mind if I saw him?" asked Betsy. It was a bold request, to visit a sick man in his bedroom, but Shelly nodded and showed her in.

"Hey there kid," said Pete.

"How you feelin' Mr. Skaggs?" she asked.

"I'll be right as rain in a day or two," he assured her. "Nice of you to check on me."

"Well Mr. Skaggs, that is one reason why I'm here. But there is another, too, a favor I need to ask," said Betsy. She went on to explain what had happened the day before, starting at the mining camp, then about the Bear Witch, and finally her conclusion about spreading scarlet fever to the village. The conversation went only slightly better than it had with Jack, but in the end Pete's kindness and sympathy for the Native Americans won out, and he agreed that they could take Sid and Top Hat to Rattlesnake Diggins.

The plan was coming together, but there was still one big hitch. Neither Betsy nor her mother knew how they would communicate with the Indians. How could they tell them they knew about the sickness, and that they had medicine? How could they explain it was safe and many had tried it and some were already recovering? How could they reassure them of their good intentions, especially if the medicine woman was there saying the opposite?

"There's an Indian miner up in camp, but I don't know what village he's from," Betsy told her mom. "We could stop by the camp on the way to the village and ask him to translate some words, but he's not very well, and I don't know how friendly he is either. He did take the Bai Hu Tang without complaint, which is better than can be said for the other men."

"I reckon the Indians are used to natural remedies," observed her mom.

"Well, I suppose that bodes well for us then," Besty said brightly. "But why should they trust us? They probably think the same of us as the old medicine woman. Who we really need is Jack Wilson."

"Jack Wilson?" asked her mom.

"Yeah, you know, the Indian we met in Nevada City, the man who healed Sid. He must be some kind of medicine man himself, but he called himself a prophet. I didn't know Indians had prophets."

"Nor did I," said her mother. "But I guess God can speak to whomever he pleases. He's God of all, not just of us white folks. That Jack Wilson seems like a good man, especially what he did for you that night. Does he live in Nevada City?"

"No, he said he's from Mason Valley. Do you know where that is?" asked Betsy.

"I think that's over the state line, a ways from here," said her mother. "If you really think he could help, you could send a telegraph."

Betsy paused. She'd never even considered a telegraph. "I can do that?"

"Sure, there's a Western Union right up in the post office in the Mountain House," her mother replied. "Probably cost us fifty cents though."

"But how would it get through to him?" asked Betsy.

"On a wing and prayer, my dear. You'd have to send it to the Mason Valley station, if they have one, and hope someone there knows who Jack Wilson is and where to find him. Then they'd deliver it.

"Mom, we've got to do it!" exclaimed Betsy. "He can help us, I know it. I've got a feeling about him."

"Well, you better write down what you want sent," said her mother.

Betsy went to a shelf and got down a piece of stationary and a pencil. She sat down at the kitchen table and began to think. She wrote on the paper:

Dear Jack Wilson. We fear an Indian village may have scarlet fever. We will take Bao's medicine to their aid. We need your help. We may run into the medicine woman. Please come to Downieville urgently. Your friend, Betsy.

She read it to her mom. "Well that's just fine, but are we going to wait for him here? I don't really think we have the time. It might take him a few days just to get the message, and another two to get up here."

Betsy slumped in her chair, but then chirped up again. "What's the fastest he could get here?" she asked hopefully.

"Well, I don't know. Two days maybe?"

"That's too long," sighed Betsy. "And I don't even know if he's in Mason Valley. He may still be in Nevada City on account of the storm."

"Then you best wire your message to Nevada City as well," said her mom.

Betsy perked up again, "Of course, I could send it to Mr. Bao. He would know how to find him. Can we spare the money?"

"I'll ask you father, but I'm sure we can," said her mother kindly.

Betsy wanted to get the telegrams off as soon as possible, so as soon as her father said okay she rushed up to the Mountain House. It was a three story building, one of the biggest in town, and served as an inn and the town's post office. Thankfully the porch was shoveled and the place was open. She found the post office clerk and asked to send a telegram via Western Union. She paid her money, which came to one dollar and twenty cents, and gave him the message and all the details. He asked for more information about Jack Wilson, so she gave them his Indian name as well, which she thankfully remembered was Wovoka. The operator sent them on the spot, using a little contraption to type out the messages in morse code, one letter at a time. They would be sent through a network of wires that had been stretched all across the United States, and somehow the message would eventually arrive in Mason Valley and Nevada City.

She knew sending the messages was the easy part. The hard part would be for the clerk on the other end to find Jack Wilson. As she walked home she kicked the snow and prayed silently it would get to him, and that he'd leave right away. Even then, she knew if her and her mother set out tomorrow for the village like they'd talked about, there was no way he'd make it in time. *Would it be right to wait for him? If they were very ill, another day could cost someone their life,* she told herself. *But no one had died up at the miner's camp, that was a good sign. Still, it didn't seem right to wait. What the village needed was the medicine, not Jack Wilson.*

When she got back home she found her father up and about, though moving slowly.

"How do you feel?" she asked as she unbundled herself from her winter coat, hat, and mittens.

"No better, no worse. I can't say if the medicine is working or not, I'm afraid. How's young Jack?" he asked.

"He's on the mend, though he doesn't think much of the mission to the Indians. Even Pete wasn't thrilled about it. He's doing about as well as you, although he's still laid up."

"Well, if this is the worst of it, then we ought to be glad," her father said. "Scarlet fever is not to be taken lightly. Did you get your telegrams sent?"

"Yes, though I don't think Jack Wilson will make it in time if we're going tomorrow. Do you think we ought to wait and see if he comes?"

"Well, I've never met this man, but I think it's a long shot," her father replied. "You don't even know if the telegram will reach him. I think it's more important you get the medicine to the village. Getting some words translated by that Indian in the mining camp was a good idea."

"Yes, I suppose your right," Betsy said reluctantly. Deep down she knew the real reason she wanted to wait for Jack Wilson was not because he might be able to help with communication, but because he could protect them from the Bear Witch. She trusted God enough to attempt the mission with her mom at her side, but not yet enough to face that white-faced woman and the bear of her nightmares.

Many miles away as the crow flies, in the Western Union office of Yerington, Nevada, the clerk transcribed the message that came over the wire. He stood up and asked a young boy to go get the deputy from the sheriff's office a block away. The boy returned with the deputy in a few minutes.

"Hey Bob, you ever heard of a Jack Wilson? Also goes by Wovoka?" the clerk asked.

"Sure, he's that washed up big-shot Indian. He's got a place somewhere north of here in the valley," replied the deputy.

"I got a telegram here for him. You know where his place is?" asked the clerk.

"I could probably find out, but if you think I'm ridin' up there to do your work, you can think again. I'm employed by the state of Nevada, not Western Union," he said, sticking his thumbs in his belt.

"Well can you tell the boy here where it is?" asked the clerk, now annoyed.

The boy looked at the clerk fearfully. He'd run telegrams around town plenty of times, but not to some strange Indian's hut in the middle of nowhere.

"Heck Bill, I don't know where it is. You can't ask this kid to find him either, you must be out of your mind," said the deputy.

The clerk looked highly annoyed now. "Fine, Mr. Jack Wilson is unavailable. Whereabouts unknown." He wadded the message up and tossed it in the trash basket next to his desk.

The message that went to Nevada City faired a bit better, thankfully. The post office clerk had done the same as the one in Yerington and beckoned the sheriff, who happened to be bored at the time and willing to walk down to Mr. Bao's store. The sheriff found it empty except for Mr. Bao himself behind the counter. He stomped the snow off his boots as the door closed behind him. Mr. Bao frowned at the pile of snow on his floor, but he knew better than to complain.

"Sorry about that old man," the sheriff said sarcastically, "but I have a telegram for a Mr. Bao. I believe that's you."

"Really?" he replied with an eyebrow raised. This was an unexpected turn of events. The sheriff sauntered over to the counter and handed over a small piece of paper. He looked around the store as if he was searching for something, then nodded to Bao and said, "Well, looks like all's in order here. Have a good day."

The sheriff tipped his hat and showed himself out as Mr. Bao read the telegram. He frowned and said to seemingly no one, "Well, this isn't for me. This is for Jack Wilson."

After a few moments and the coast was clear, Jack Wilson rose from behind the counter where he'd been crouching out of sight. He straightened his vest, and Mr. Bao handed him the telegram.

Jack Wilson squinted at it and handed it back. "I can't read," he said in his characteristic baritone voice.

CHAPTER 17

BACK INTO THE COLD

§

The plan was set. Tomorrow morning they would pack some light provisions and walk to the Skagg's place. They'd saddle Sid and Top Hat and head back to the mining camp. Betsy had prepared a list of words they hoped the Indian there would help them translate, presuming he was of the same tribe as the village at Rattlesnake Diggins. Betsy would see if the doctor had any Bai Hu Tang left to add to her own small supply in case the village needed it.

From the camp they'd backtrack slightly to where Betsy and Jack had headed up into the mountains on the day they met the medicine woman. They'd follow the ridge until they came into view of the village, and then make their way down into the valley.

Then came the part Betsy was most nervous about: entering the village. They had no real plan except to ride into the village and try to communicate their intentions with whomever appeared. They presumed being female would aid their cause. They certainly didn't appear threatening, not in the way two men would. If they were successful, they'd administer medicine to whomever needed it.

Presently Betsy lay in bed thinking about what tomorrow would bring. She was nervous, and there were multiple reasons. She didn't know what would happen if the Bear Witch showed up. She was nervous they wouldn't be able to communicate. She was nervous they'd both be shot with arrows within one hundred feet of the village. And she was nervous she'd have nightmares about it all as soon as she closed her eyes.

She fought off her nerves by going through the plan over and over again, trying to think of ways to improve their odds. One thing she knew about plans was that they rarely worked. Her plan to frame the gold thieves and have them arrested had not gone at all like she'd expected, and there was no reason to think this new plan would either. What was their plan 'B' if plan 'A' didn't work? Run, she supposed. Run and hope they don't shoot arrows in their backs. If only Jack Wilson miraculously appeared on their doorstep in the morning, that would make her feel so much better, but she knew there was little chance of such luck.

The weakness in their plan, she thought, was entering the village. They needed some way to convey they were friendly, that they were there to help. What they needed, she thought, was a *welcoming gift.*

Of course! A peace offering! Isn't that what Indians did when they met with white men?

Then, out of the blue, she thought of the perfect thing. She threw off her covers and jumped out of bed. She opened her bedroom door, marched out into living room, picked up the Harper's Weekly from the side table, and walked into the kitchen where her mother was finishing up the day's chores.

"Mom, I've got it," she pronounced.

Her mom stopped her scrubbing and looked at Betsy curiously. "You've got what?"

"We need a peace offering, for when we first come into the village. A way to let the Indians know we come in peace."

"Yes?" her mother said slowly.

Betsy laid Harper's Weekly on the counter and pointed with her finger at the Christmas tree.

"That's what we need," said Betsy. "Think about it, it's a natural symbol of peace they can understand. Certainly they love trees as much as we do. We decorate it with beads and baubles, which is what Indians like to do, too - you know, with all their beads and feathers and what not?"

"And how are we going to get a Christmas tree up to Rattlesnake Diggins?" asked her mother.

"I thought of that too. Sid and Top Hat pulled a big sled all the way from Nevada City. Well, that wouldn't make it up the ridge. Mr. Fairlane is working on making it convertible so it can be a sleigh in winter and a wagon in the summer, but he's not done yet. But it did give me an idea: Molly has a little runner sled, you know the one she got last year for Christmas? We can use that to drag the tree into the village. That would be nothin' for Sid, he can pull it right up the ridge. Once we're in eye shot of the village, we can tie the horses up and walk down with Molly's sled and the Christmas tree right into the middle of it. Surely then they'd know we're coming with good intentions!"

"Well, it's not a bad idea…" her mother said thoughtfully. "It's going to take some time though, to find a tree and decorate it, don't you think?"

"Not at all, we can stop by Molly's on the way out tomorrow, I'm sure she'll say yes to letting us borrow her sled, and find a little pine sapling on the way. We only need to round up some decorations, and we can do that right now!'" exclaimed Betsy, looking around the kitchen.

"Hmmm, yes. We'll have to be creative I suppose, we don't have any Christmas ornaments like that," said her mother, eyeing the magazine.

Their life in Downieville was a simple one without extravagance. The frontier didn't allow them to afford luxuries. Their Christmas decorations usually amounted to a handmade wreath on the door and a second wreath set with four advent candles which they set on their dining table. That was it.

"Don't you have some beads or buttons or something we could use?" asked Betsy.

"Let me check my sewing box," said her mother, getting up to go into the front room. "I have some red ribbon we could make some bows out of…"

"Perfect! What can we use as a garland to drape around it?" asked Betsy.

"Well, I have some thread, but…"

"I've got it," interrupted Betsy. "Popcorn! I'll pop some corn and we can use a needle to run the thread through and make a garland!

I'm sure I've seen that somewhere."

Betsy and her mother stayed up late that night creating decorations from whatever brightly colored objects they could find around the house. Her mother tied bows using red ribbon. They tied buttons loops of thread. Betsy popped two batches of corn in a pot on the stove and spent an hour threading it into a garland. She threaded little red berries from a bush behind their house intermittently to add some Christmas color.

At about one o'clock in the morning they placed all their decorations on the kitchen table and surveyed them with satisfaction.

"A shame we can't keep all this for our own," said Betsy, proud of their creations.

Her mother wrapped her arm around her neck and said, "'Tis better to give than receive. That's the spirit of Christmas!"

Betsy went to bed with a warm feeling of Christmas cheer. She held onto that feeling and let her mind imagine their happy arrival in the Indian village tomorrow, men, women, and children coming out into the snow to see the unusual but merry sight of a Christmas tree for the first time, smiles creeping on to their faces. She envisioned going into one of the huts and finding the boy she'd seen sick in bed, boiling water over a little fire, boiling the medicine, and helping him drink the tea that would make him feel better. She held these thoughts as tightly as a she could as she drifted towards sleep, hoping they'd carry over into her dreams. And that night, with her heart filled with the joyful spirit of Christmas, which was really just the spirit of generosity and love, the Spirit of Jesus himself, the nightmares did not come. Those fears and doubts were silenced by a greater power, and Betsy slept sound as a baby.

Dawn broke over the Sierra Nevada mountains the next morning with none of its usual grandeur. Wintery clouds still enshrouded the California wilderness and a heavy fog had settled in the valleys and swales. In this fog sat Jack Wilson, bolt upright, as still as a statue. He sat below a rock outcropping that could've almost been a cave had it been any deeper. This was his temporary camp, and it lay just west of Nevada City. The remains of a campfire smoldered four feet from where he sat, legs crisscrossed.

He'd sat in this position without moving a muscle for the last nine hours, with only a woven blanket and the fire for warmth. Now, with the morning's first light, his skin had gone blue with cold. The only one around to see this peculiar sight was his horse, which was tied to a tree twenty feet away.

This was not the first time Jack Wilson, or Wovoka as we rightly ought to call him, had been in such a trance. The same had happened that day in the forest when he was cutting wood, when the Great Father had given him his vision of the afterlife and told him to carry his message of peace to all of his people. It had happened since then as well, and others had observed it. White men, who were naturally skeptical of native American spirituality, would later recount to others that what they'd witnessed had been no stunt. The man was truly as rigid as a board, immovable, and seemingly in another world. It was during these strange trances that his visions would come.

What Wovoka saw that night was this: there was a Bear hunting fish in a river. She was fat, ready for her hibernation, but she kept hunting, as bears do before the long winter months. A Coyote and a Cougar were on either side of the Bear, and they watched from a distance. The Cougar had a cub with her, who also watched the Bear catching fish. The Bear was wary of the Coyote and the Cougar, for she knew they wished to steal her fish. But the Coyote was clever. It spoke to the Bear and said, "the Cougar wants to steal your fish, kill it so that it will no longer threaten you."

So the Bear charged the Cougar and they fought, claws out and fangs bared. The Bear was larger and stronger and angrier, and soon the mother Cougar was overcome. While they fought, the little cub saw the Coyote come and steal the bear's fish and disappear into the woods. And then the little cub saw its mother lying on the ground. The little cub said to the Bear, "What have you done? While you were fighting, the Coyote has stolen all your fish!"

Then, in his vision, the earth began to shake and the ground opened up between the Bear and the cub. The voice of the Earth Creator came from the ground with a mighty rumble and spoke solemnly saying, "This must stop." But the Bear, seeing her fish had been stolen and hearing the Earth Creator speak against her, only became more enraged, and it charged the cub. Wovoka could stand no more, and he stepped in front of the cub and said, "Stop your fighting! Live in peace! So says the Earth Creator!"

When Wovoka woke from his vision he was very stiff and very cold. It took a few minutes for him to make his body move again. He stood up slowly, in pain, for the cold had seeped into his very bones. Despite the cold, he did not stoke the fire to warm himself. Instead, he went to his horse, untied it, and climbed on. He leaned forward and whispered something in his native tongue, then turned the horse towards the trail that lead up to the road. The horse worked the cold out of its joints as it jolted its way through the snow up the trail. When they emerged onto the road, Wovoka turned his horse to the north and urged it into a gallop, a cold wind in his face.

Twenty four miles yonder the Wescott household was awake and preparing for their journey. Even Betsy's father was up, making them breakfast. He moved slowly, but with purpose. He wanted to see them off with what little energy he had, though he was sad and a little ashamed he wasn't going himself. They packed their few provisions, a saw for the tree, and some jute rope to tow it with and tie it to the sled. Betsy stowed their decorations carefully in a second bag, then they bundled themselves up in their coats, hats, mittens and boots. They took extra blankets on Betsy's recommendation, which they wrapped around their shoulders.

Reverend Wescott gathered his wife and daughter around him, placed his hands on their shoulders, and prayed for their journey, the Indians, the medicine, the horses, on and on until Betsy got a little restless. Finally he said 'Amen,' and they were soon out the door, back into the cold.

CHAPTER 18

HOW TO ENTER AN INDIAN VILLAGE

§

The snow had finally stopped, though the sun had not yet returned. Instead, low gray clouds hurried by above them, carrying the possibility of more snow with them. Betsy looked up and down the street, hoping her big native American friend had somehow got her message and miraculously made it to Downieville overnight, but the only living thing in sight was one of the town dogs sniffing a fencepost.

Betsy and her mother walked to Pete's place and saddled up their horses, Sid and Top Hat, then headed to Molly's. Betsy's mother did not ride much, but she'd lived in the West long enough to know how to handle a horse better than most women of their day. She expertly dismounted at Molly's, lashed her horse to the front rail, and knocked on the door.

Mrs. Cooper, Molly's mother, answered, and the two women traded greetings. Molly's mother welcomed them inside and asked how Reverend Wescott was. Betsy's mother reassured her that he was improving, thanks in part to the medicine that Betsy and Jack had retrieved from Nevada City. When they finally got around to the business of borrowing the sled, Molly had appeared. As Betsy's mother explained their mission, Molly's eyes grew wide. Mrs. Cooper put her hand to her mouth in polite astonishment.

"Well of course you can borrow Molly's sled for such a noble mission, but are you sure it's safe?" asked Mrs. Cooper.

"We are in the hands of our Lord, Mrs. Cooper," replied Betsy's mother with a confident smile. "I feel there's no safer place to be."

"Yes, but with what's gone on recently, not to mention this snow..." Mrs. Cooper's voice trailed off.

"All taken under consideration, Mrs. Cooper. Though we'll happily accept your prayers," Betsy's mother stated calmly.

Molly put on her overcoat and went outside with Betsy to fetch the sled from around back. It was not unlike one of our modern Flexible Flyer runner sleds, but the runners were made of thick wooden spars that came to a point in the front, and it stood higher off the ground. It was just big enough for two children, or one small Christmas tree.

The Coopers saw the Wescotts off, waving farewells, and soon Betsy and her mother were clopping along the road that lead north out of Downieville with a small sled in tow. They kept their eye out for a pine sapling, which provided a nice distraction from the unknown that lay ahead. Once they'd passed the town limits it didn't take long for Betsy to spot a young tree. She hopped down, handed the reins to her mother, grabbed the saw and plowed through the snow up the hill to where it stood.

"It's a little skinny compared to the one in the picture," Betsy yelled back. "It doesn't have a lot of branches." She circled the tree and evaluated it.

"I don't think you'll find one like the magazine up here," returned her mother.

Betsy came running back down in her tracks to the road. "I think we should keep looking for a better one."

They went another five hundred yards and stopped again. Betsy had spotted another one.

"This one's a bit sparse on one side," she called down.

"Well, you'll have to pick one, or else we'll be out here 'til dark," came her mother's reply.

But Betsy wanted the perfect tree, so she came back down and they kept looking. This happened two more time until finally, on the fifth attempt, her mother's protests won out, and Betsy compromised with a somewhat thin pine sapling just taller than she was. She had the saw through the trunk in no time and was soon dragging it down to the horses.

"I think it looks lovely," said her mother as she dismounted to help Betsy tie it to the sled. There was no use decorating yet, that would need to wait until they got up on the ridge. They managed to get the rope around the trunk and secure it without damaging any branches.

Their next stop was the mining camp at Hank's Bluff. Betsy led her mother past the old mill, over Pauley Creek and then up the long climb to the camp. This time there were two men up and about, a

155

good sign Betsy thought. They recognized "nurse" Besty from two days before and tipped their hats. Betsy and her mother tied the horses to a tree and made their way over to the main mess tent. The men had trod well defined paths in the snow around camp, another sign that people must be recovering, she thought. Betsy lifted the flap and poked her head in. *Where was Dr. Marten?*

Clancy spotted Betsy and stood from a chair where he sat. Betsy saw the man he was attending to laying in the cot was the doctor. He'd finally been struck by the fever.

"Hello there Nurse Betsy," said Clancy, nodding politely to the two of them

"This is my mother, Mary," said Betsy with a nervous smile.

"Mrs. Wescott, nice to see you" Clancy said respectfully, recognizing her from church. "The doc came down with it hard yesterday, he's been out ever since."

"Did he take more of the medicine?" asked Betsy.

"Yes, he did yesterday, but not this morning. Said he don't want to use it all up," Clancy replied.

"It's good of you to take care of him," said Betsy's mother to Clancy.

"It's the right thing to do, ma'am," the little Irishman replied.

"Mr. Clancy, is that Indian man still here?" asked Betsy.

"You must mean Injin' Joe," replied Clancy. "'Fraid not. He's done run off again, ain't seen him since he started feelin' better. Did you mean to check in on him?"

"Oh, well yes, in a manner. But if he's not here, then, well," she looked at her mother.

Betsy's mother came to her aid. "That's quite alright Mr. Clancy, it wasn't anything pressing. Now, is there anything the camp needs? If there's something, we can have it run up here tomorrow."

"That's very kind Mrs. Wescott. Food was getting' a little thin, but Carl went to town yesterday and fetched some grub. We're doin' okay now. Some men have got better and Barley has already got 'em back in the mine. He said I was to stay back and look after the rest, though your daughter here is far better suited to nursin' than myself."

"It looks like you're doing a fine job, Mr. Clancy," replied her mother kindly. "Well, if the camp is well stocked and there's nothing needed, we'll be on our way."

Clancy bid them a polite farewell as they turned and left. As soon as they were out of the tent, Betsy burst out, "What now, ma? How are we going to talk to the Indians if we don't know any words?"

"We'll just have to use sign language. If we're lucky maybe someone there will know some English. Many Indians do these days," her mother reassured her as they walked back to the horses.

"I don't know, ma, I got a bad feelin' all the sudden," Betsy said worriedly. The plan was falling apart before her very eyes, and they'd barely begun.

An hour later Betsy and her mother sat on their horses high on the snow-covered ridge that overlooked the little Maidu village and stared down into what seemed to them a completely different world. They'd not had any trouble finding their way, Betsy had remembered the ridge and they'd soon encountered the tracks that the medicine woman and her bear had left two days before. They'd stopped to pick up the grey blanket she'd thrown down and spit on, the same one Betsy had dropped from the wagon on their way to Nevada City.

Now, below them was the peculiar sight of twelve large mounds of snow, smoke drifting up from most of them, footpaths weaving in between. Betsy scanned the village and the surrounding valley for any signs of a bear and found none. Good news as this was, it didn't seem to loosen the knot that had formed in her stomach.

It was up on that ridge, in the face of a blustery winter wind, that Betsy decorated her very first Christmas tree, and every Christmas tree she would decorate from that day on would remind her of this day. First, they wrapped the rope around the base of the trunk a good many times, and then under the seat of the sled, then around again, and under again, until the stump was fixed securely. Next, they cut the rope and used shorter pieces as guy lines, tying them mid-way up the trunk and down to the corners of the sled. They shook the tree to test it, and it held firm. Finally they tied a tow rope to the back of the sled so that they could lower it down the hill, one in front, one behind, without it getting away from them.

With the rope work complete, they started decorating their little tree with the buttons and bows they'd crafted the night before. Though it should have been a joyful experience, Betsy's mother could read the worry in her face as they tied hanging buttons on the sprigs of the tree.

"I wonder if this is what Mary and Joseph felt as they came into

Bethlehem the night the Savior was born?" Betsy's mother asked to calm their nerves. "Can you imagine being pregnant with no place to stay? That must've been real scary for a young girl like her."

Betsy remained silent. She didn't feel like small talk. That evil woman could be in one of those huts below her, and rather than running away, she was running in.

"I think it looks lovely," said her mother as they finished draping the garland around the tree. "I really like the red berries you added."

They put the finishing touches on the tree and stood for a moment, admiring it. The green branches of the little tree were now delightfully decorated with colorful buttons, red bows, and the elegantly draped popcorn garland. It didn't quite look like the picture on Harper's Weekly, but it was enough to bring a meager smile to Betsy's face.

"Are you ready?" asked her mother.

"Not really," she said softly, looking down at the village.

Her mother began to pray out loud, "Dear Father above, we ask your hand to guide us and your voice to speak through us to the people we shall meet soon. Protect us and keep us as we lend aid to those who need it. We do all for your glory, in Jesus' name we pray, Amen."

Betsy patted Sid on the neck and said, "We'll be back shortly boy." Then she picked up the front tow line and her mother picked up the rear. They started down, Betsy forging a new path through the windblown snow. The ridge sloped away from them sharply, but if they walked diagonally down and to their right, they'd be able to keep

159

the tree on the sled upright and eventually they'd come to the little creek at the bottom, across which lay the edge of the village. The ridge was protected by trees, but further down, the slope got steeper and the trees ended. The final approach to the village was right out in the open.

They managed the first part of the descent with no problems. Her mother kept the rear line tight and tree bumped along in Betsy's tracks. When they came to the steep, open part, Betsy paused. This was it. Her stomach churned inside her and it felt like fear was choking her with cold hands around her neck.

"I think we can zig zag down this part, it's too steep to head straight down," said her mother.

Betsy nodded and stepped out from the cover of the trees into the open snow of the valley side. As she did, she heard what at first sounded like the call of crow, but something wasn't right. It wasn't a crow, but a human call, a warning call from a lookout.

Of course, there would be a lookout, and now they'd been spotted. The call continued, the sound moving, getting closer, coming down the ridge from above them. The crow call turned into what sounded like an Indian battle cry.

"Keep going," urged her mother from behind. "They'll see we mean no harm soon enough."

They kept moving downward, Betsy taking big steps, and with each one the snow slid out from under her a little. Her mother was sliding behind her as well. Then, from out of the trees above and to their right burst the Indian scout, his overcoat made of fur pelts flying from his shoulders, feathers waving in his hair, a stout stick in his hand. The snow exploded before him as he raced in their direction, crying his terrible war cry, his arm raised with his stick ready to strike.

At that moment, her mother's footing gave way and she slipped backwards. The rope fell from her hands and the sled took off forward towards Betsy. She leaned uphill and tried to catch it, grabbing the legs of the runners, but her footing gave as well and soon she was sliding on her belly, holding onto the rear of the sled pointing downhill. Her blanket slid off her shoulders and snow was flying in her face and down the front of her coat. Somehow in the chaos of her downward slide, she pushed her elbows up and spit snow out of her mouth, gasping for air. She could see the creek below her getting larger rapidly, as well as something to her right in her peripheral vision. She looked and saw the Indian barreling down the hill next to her, still upright somehow, snow flying in all directions, but completely out of control, just as she was. Then, for a split second, he looked at Betsy. Their eyes met, both wide as pie plates, and the two of them realized they were in the same predicament, at the mercy of the mountain, their only hope of survival the two feet of soft, cushioning snow at the base of the hill.

Betsy's mother had not slid, but watched from above as her daughter and the Indian scout fell like an avalanche away from her. In the village below she saw a few heads poke out from their huts just as the fury of snow reached the bottom. She could see the slope rise before it ended in the creek, and she put her hand to her mouth as

Betsy and the Indian crested the rise and went flying through the air, arcing over the creek, Christmas tree first, followed by Betsy holding on for dear life, and the Indian right next to her. Somehow the Christmas tree landed upright and kept going, but Betsy could not hold on during the impact and she and the Indian tumbled to a stop on the other side of the creek. The Christmas tree slid right into the middle of the village and stopped, perfectly upright.

Down below, Betsy lifted her head from the snow. It had been a soft landing, and she hoped her fellow traveler had faired as well as she had. He was lying just five feet away, looking at her. For a moment, both just lay there, astonished. If you've ever been sledding downhill in winter time, you'll know what came next. You'll know because it's impossible not to do what they both did. Betsy was not sure who started it, but soon they were smiling and a second later, they were both laughing! Deep, soul-filled belly laughs!

CHAPTER 19

FROM LAUGHTER TO TRAGEDY

§

After watching the crash at the bottom of the slope, Betsy's mother had come straight down the hill in a panic, nearly as fast as the Indian. She stopped where their tracks left the snow on the crest before the creek and only then heard the laughter. Her heart leapt with relief and she sat back in the snow. She couldn't help but join in. The villagers who'd seen the tail end of the disaster were laughing, too, and gathering around Betsy and their lookout.

More and more people came out of their huts to see what the commotion was about. The young man who was the lookout began talking to them animatedly, pointing his stick up the hill, telling what had happened. While he told the story, they watched Mary Wescott in her long winter dress gingerly make her way across the little creek and join Betsy at the edge of the village.

For a while, there was an awkward confusion, as the Maidu tried to figure out why there were two white women suddenly in their village, along with a strangely decorated pine sapling. They talked excitedly amongst themselves and stared at their visitors, unsure what to do next. Betsy and her mother stood there in their dresses and long coats, smiling warmly, before Betsy finally spoke.

"Hello friends," she said slowly. "We bring medicine if any are sick."

Betsy and Mary looked around hopefully for any sign of understanding, but there were only confused stares. One man had made his way to the front of the gathering. He held the respect of the rest, and Betsy assumed he was the chief. Maidu villages often had multiple elders, not just one, but this man clearly held some authority. When he spoke, all listened. He called for someone and soon a man came forward, making his way through the group. He was not dressed like the rest, and immediately Betsy recognized him from the mining camp. It was the man they called Injin' Joe, though his real English name was Joseph.

"He wants to know why you here," said Joseph in broken English.

Betsy and Mary were never so happy to hear their own language.

"We come peacefully and to share medicine to any who might be sick," said Betsy.

Joseph turned and translated this to the chief. The chief nodded sternly and then spoke more to the man. The man replied, and there ensued a long conversation between the two, which all listened to with rapt attention. Betsy and Mary could only watch and wonder.

Finally, Joseph turned to them and said, "The sickness has come to our village too. Two families remain in their huts. I tell chief about you and your medicine. I tell him you gave medicine to me and the sickness leave. He not trust me because I go away to work for white man. He does not want white man's medicine."

Betsy removed from her bag the satchel of Bai Hu Tang. She poured some of the dried mixture into her hand and showed everyone. "This is old medicine. One thousand years old. It comes from roots, just like your medicine. We boil it, and then drink. My father has drunk it, too. We have all become well again. Please let me give it to your sick."

Joseph turned and translated to the chief. He looked down at Besty and her medicine and thought for a moment. Then he spoke again, turned and left.

"He will ask the shaman what to do," said Joseph.

Betsy watched the chief walk towards the far side of the village. On the outskirts of the main village was a hut that appeared a little different than the rest. Three long ceremonial sticks stood in the snow by the entrance, decorated with feathers and beaded string. On the top of the center stick was the bleached white skull of an elk or deer, also decorated with feathers. The chief pulled back a fur pelt and disappeared inside the hut.

For a few minutes Betsy and the villagers stood in silence, waiting for the chief to reemerge. Joseph said, "the shaman is also sick with the fever."

Then the chief reappeared from the hut. He held the fur pelt aside, and out came an old woman, hunched over so that Betsy could not see her face. She looked weak and frail, and began coughing violently, still hunched over. The chief held her arm, steadying her, and then she looked up. Betsy saw her face. The white paint was smudged and faded, but her eyes were unmistakable.

The old woman took a moment for her eyes to adjust to the light. She looked around the huts and then at the people she knew. When she saw Betsy and her mother, her expression changed, her eyes narrowed, and her posture straightened. She seemed to suddenly gain a foot in stature, her shoulders becoming proud. She stepped forward and pointed a bony finger at Betsy. The villagers backed away from Betsy, as if distancing themselves from a curse.

The old woman began to yell in her native tongue those same horrible sounding words that had haunted Betsy's dreams. Betsy cowered next to her mother, who stepped forward protectively.

"What's she saying?" Betsy's mother asked Joseph.

"She says this is the white girl who brought the sickness. She says leave at once," he replied.

The medicine woman pulled one of the ceremonial sticks from the snow and started coming towards them, shouting and waving her stick in the air. Her frailty had disappeared, her weakness had turned to strength, fueled by anger. The other Maidu watched as she came forward, backing away further. None stepped forward to intercede, even Joseph retreated. Betsy and her mother stood still, their hearts beating madly.

Just ten feet now separated them from the shaman woman. Betsy was physically shaking, holding on to her mother. The woman glared at them, then began yelling new words, her voice somehow greater and more violent than the aging body from which it came. Then, in a sudden frenzy, the shaman rushed at them with her stick. Mary sprang into action, grabbing the stick with both hands. She pivoted and forced the stick to her right, away from Betsy, who'd fallen to the ground, her knees giving way in fright. The old woman did not fall, but braced herself with unnatural strength. She screamed something and pushed violently again, unbalancing Mary who staggered backwards but didn't lose grip of the stick. They were locked with the stick between them, but somehow the old woman was overpowering her.

Betsy watched in horror as the ghost of her nightmares seemed to amass the supernatural strength of a bear, surging suddenly forward and sending her mother tumbling backwards onto her back in the snow. The old woman was now on top of her, only the stick between them.

Betsy was panic stricken. Her legs would not move. Her mouth would not let her cry for help. She looked in desperation to the villagers, surely someone would help, someone would step in and save her mother, but they only stared in shock. The old woman had a power they would not dare challenge.

And then it began. Betsy thought her world was ending when it started. The earth felt as though it was shaking, and she thought to herself that this must be how it feels to see your mother die. But the earth felt like it was shaking because it *was* shaking. Betsy only realized this because the villagers were suddenly distracted from the fight between the shaman and her mother and were staring at the ground first, and then up at the hills. The trees quivered and snow began falling from their branches all at once.

Then there came a loud voice. It was an Indian voice in an Indian language, but she could understand it clear as day. It said powerfully, "Stop this! Stop fighting!" The voice was the chief's, and he now stood next to the shaman. He grabbed her by the shoulder and flung her off Betsy's mother.

The old woman glared at the chief in disbelief. She'd never been challenged. Her eyes grew wide, and for a moment Betsy didn't know if she was about to charge him, but then the earth shook again and his voice boomed, "So says the Earth Creator!"

All the people around the village gasped. There was no mistaking it, the Earth Creator had spoken, for the ground had pronounced it. Then the scariest thing of all happened. The old woman, whose spirit was so filled with rage, realized the Creator *had* spoken against her, and the anger that had fueled her rage was suddenly replaced by fear. The power she'd used against others came round about and now stared her straight in the face, shaking the ground and speaking with an authority beyond any earthly being. This was a power greater than any she'd ever known, a power to be feared, so stark and present that her frail body could not bear it. Her eyes, which were still staring wide at the chief, rolled back in her head, her body went limp, and she died. The Creator had given life, and the Creator had taken life.

When Betsy saw Kapam-Kylem die, for that was her name, she felt a weight lift from her body. Strength returned to her shaking knees, and she rose to her feet. The sense of dread that had filled her when she watched Kapam-Kylem emerge from her hut was gone, replaced by an overwhelming sensation of gratefulness and appreciation to the Creator, the name these people used for God. Everyone around her was silent as she went and knelt to tend to her mother, who still lay in the snow. The people watched as Betsy gently helped Mary sit up.

The chief suddenly called out, "Moon Dog and Flying-High Hawk, come take Bear Woman to her house. Cover her with rabbit-pelts. Tomorrow morning we will start the great Cry."

Betsy didn't know how she could suddenly understand the Maidu language, but it did not strike her as strange at the time. She somehow knew that it was the power of the Great Spirit, the Holy Spirit as she and her mother knew it, that was giving her a special gift.

Moon Dog and Flying-High Hawk soon appeared. Moon Dog paused by the chief and asked "What about them?" pointing to Betsy and her mother.

"They must leave now," he said forcefully. "Dirt Face, tell them to go. We do not want their medicine." The name given to Joseph was one of disrespect and double meaning. His face was often dirty from working in the mines.

Joseph reappeared and began to translate to Betsy, but she stopped him and stood to her feet. She faced the chief squarely and looked him in the eye. Her expression was not forceful, but generous and confident. When she opened her mouth, Maidu words came out that she did not know herself.

"He'i helin To si dum, Ko'doyapem wewen," she said. When

the people around her heard their own language, there was a collective gasp of astonishment. The chief's eyebrows raised and he listened intently as Betsy went on speaking in the Maidu language:

"You need not fear the white people, nor the arrows that fly by day, nor the plague that stalks in the dark. If you live in the shelter of the Great Father and make your home in the shadow of the Almighty Creator, you can say to Him, "My refuge, my fortress, my God in whom I trust.

"He rescues you from the snares of the fowlers hoping to destroy you; he covers you with his feathers and you find shelter under his wings. The Great Father says:

I rescue all who cling to me,

I protect whoever knows my name,

I answer everyone who calls on me,

I am with them when they are in trouble;

I bring them safety and honor,

I give them life, long and full, and show them how I can save."

All those who witnessed this were amazed, not the least of which the chief. Betsy could hear them begin to murmur while the chief considered what to do next. Then he spoke and they went silent.

"Earth Creator has spoken today, first through my voice, and now through this girl's voice," he said. "Let her give her medicine to the sick. It is good medicine. Take them to the sick."

Betsy smiled and a wave of joy seemed to pass through her body, giving her goosebumps. Those were the last Maidu words that Betsy would understand, for the Indian scout stepped forward and volunteered to take them, but the words he spoke were unintelligible. He beckoned for Betsy and Mary to follow him. Mary, having observed the miraculous conversation between Betsy and the chief, found herself strangely calmed. She regathered herself and rose to her feet.

"Joseph, can you join us to translate?" she asked with remarkable composure.

"We need to boil water," said Betsy to Joseph. Joseph seemed to understand this and related this request to one of the women standing nearby, who nodded and went away.

The lookout, whose Indian name was translated Running-Water, led them to one of the huts and pushed aside the hanging pelt in the low doorway. He crouched outside and spoke words into the hut. He repeated them, then added more, for those inside had not witnessed what had occurred outside.

"He says a medicine woman has arrived to the village," translated Joseph. "He says she is white skinned and young, but has good medicine." Joseph leaned in to hear the response from whomever was in the hut.

"He asks where Kapam-Kylem is," said Joseph, which Running-Water pondered for a moment. In their culture, the medicine woman's most important role was healing.

"She not well," was Running-Water's delayed reply. "Chief Broad-Mountain says to take white girl's medicine. It is good medicine."

Finally there was a word from inside the hut and Running-Water nodded for Betsy and her mother to enter.

"Aren't you going in?" asked Betsy to Running-Water. Joseph translated and Running-Water shook his head no.

"Of course, the fever," said Betsy. She turned to her mom and said, "You shouldn't come in either. I can do this. I did it with the miners."

Her mother smiled and said, "I have every confidence in you. And look, here comes the hot water!"

The Maidu woman brought the water over in a pot. Betsy made a cupping shape with her hands and brought it to her mouth. The woman caught her meaning and returned a minute later with a cup hand-carved from wood.

It took a few minutes more to prepare the medicine, and then it was time. Betsy was about to enter the home of an Indian, and she had no idea what to expect inside. She plucked up her courage, ducked her head, and went in.

CHAPTER 20

HEALING THE SICK

§

Betsy went through the low door. Two things hit her immediately: it was boiling hot inside and it smelled of campfire. Her eyes adjusted to the low light and she first saw a man propped up on a bed of pine needs covered by a colorful blanket. Beads of sweat covered his face and arms. His wife was next to him with her eyes half open, her skin red with rash. Betsy could tell she was feverish.

To their right on another, smaller bed was a young boy whom Betsy thought could be the same one she'd seen on the road five days before. He was asleep. She could see the rash all over his arms. In the center of the hut, which was round and supported by dozens of heavy branches, there was a stack of rocks that formed a kind of loose fitting igloo with a fire burning inside. It was this primitive oven that was creating the sauna-like atmosphere.

Betsy wasn't sure if it would be appropriate to remove her coat, so instead she went and quietly knelt in front of the man. He watched her every move closely, studying her white skin and fair, reddish blonde hair. He very well might of thought he was in some fever-induced dream. To see this young stranger in his home pouring some strange smelling water into a cup was beyond anything he could have imagined at that moment.

She gave the first cup of medicine to the man and motioned for him to drink. He slowly brought it to his lips and then boldly drank it all down in one sudden move. He frowned at the taste as he handed the cup back.

Betsy smiled and poured more, indicating it was for his wife. He turned over and woke her. He spoke a few soft words to her and helped her to sit up. Betsy handed the cup to the man and he helped his wife drink it down a few sips at a time.

Betsy was starting to sweat herself by this point. *Why was it a million degrees in here?* She could bear it no longer and removed her coat, wiping her arm across her perspiring brow. The man smiled at this and spoke some Indian words to her. She imagined it was a joke of sorts, and she smiled back.

She motioned toward the boy who was sleeping. The man understood and rose from the bed. Betsy averted her eyes. He wore almost no clothing, but the man didn't seem embarrassed in the least. He knelt next to his son to rouse him, and the boy stirred and slowly woke.

When the boy saw Betsy his eyes grew wide. He put up one hand as a friendly greeting to her. His father spoke some words to him, likely explaining why she was there. She poured out one more cupful of the medicine, and his father gave it to him to drink, which he did with only a little sign of distaste.

"Hello," the boy said.

"Oh! Do you know how to speak English?" she returned excitedly.

The boy looked a little anxious all the sudden and he shook his
head. "Joseph teach," he said clumsily.

"Ah, Joseph has taught you some English," she replied approv-
ingly.

"Yes, words taught me some Joseph!" he said.

Betsy laughed.

"Medicine," she said, pointing to the cup in his hands.

"Med-i-cine," repeated the boy.

"Good!" she smiled.

"Good!" said the boy. His father and mother were both smiling
as well by now.

"Feel better soon," she said.

The boy looked confused at this. He didn't understand.

"Medicine makes sickness go away," offered Betsy.

The boy nodded hopefully this time. "Sick-ness go away.
Good!" he said.

"Yes!" laughed Betsy. "Sickness go away. Then you and me
visit again." As she said this she pointed to him and then her and
motioned with her hands, but the boy looked confused again.

She tried again, "Sickness go away and you and me play games
together."

"Sickness go away...play games?" the boy asked.

"Yes!" said Betsy as she tried to quickly think of some game.
"Swim!" she said, making the motion for swimming, then "Run!" as

she ran in place, then "Catch!" she said, motioning to throw something at him, and then finally, "Dance!" she said, taking his hands and tapping her feet in a kind of play dance.

The boy smiled and looked at his parents nervously. They were more confused than he.

"Oh golly, what am I saying?" said Betsy, now embarrassed. But the boy was getting the idea of some kind of celebration, and he stood and did a little Indian dance of his own, which made Besty laugh. She really wanted to visit the boy again, but she didn't know how to put it in a way they'd understand. Finally, she just said plainly, "I'm glad to meet you. What is your name?"

The boy understood at least the question and replied, "Skipping-Rock."

"My name is Betsy, and I hope to see you again," she said with a little curtsy.

"Bet-see," he repeated.

"Yes, Betsy. I hope to see you again," she said.

"See you again," the boy repeated with what appeared to be at least a glimmer of understanding.

Betsy smiled widely. "Goodbye Skipping-Rock."

"Good-bye Bet-see," he said.

"Good!" she said and turned to his parents. She curtsied and said, "Good-bye" again, to which the man replied in his best English, "Good-bye."

She took the cup and the pot of medicine and ducked out the low door. The winter air outside felt colder than ever. She shivered and suddenly remembered, "Oh my goodness, my coat!"

She ducked back in to the amusement of Skipping-Rock and his parents, grabbed her coat, curtsied one more time, and left. Back outside she quickly put on her coat and said to Joseph with a blush, "It's mighty warm in there!"

"Indians believe sweat removes sickness," he said, then relayed the equivalent words to Running-Water who was watching Betsy and her mother with great amusement.

"Sweat good medicine!" said Running-Water to the surprise of Betsy and Mary. He grinned when he saw he'd impressed them, though he knew little English. He was only fitting words together as he heard them used, but he was clearly a fast learner.

"Oh, and one more thing," said Betsy to Joseph. "Next time you talk to Skipping-Rock, tell him I want to visit him when he's feeling better. I tried to tell him, but I don't think he understood."

Joseph was beginning to like Betsy and reassured her that he would.

Running-Water took them to another hut, leant into the doorway and had a similar conversation to the one he'd had with Skipping-Rock's parents. When he'd finished explaining, Running-Water nodded to Betsy and she went in, this time finding a girl and her mother. This hut was much like the last, with the same stone oven and overwhelming heat. Betsy took off her coat right away. She did her best to smile and put her patients at ease, but the mother looked frightened. She kept speaking to Running-Water, who continued to reassure her from just outside the doorway.

The girl was younger than Skipping-Rock and looked very feverish. She was less alert and looked weak and listless. Of all the cases she'd seen at the miner's camp and at home, this one was the worst. She poured out the medicine in front the mother like she'd done previously and motioned to drink it. She offered it to the mother, but she resisted. Betsy motioned again, and reluctantly the mother drank a sip, frowning at the taste. Betsy motioned to drink more, and eventually the woman finished the cup.

Betsy then leant over to the little girl, indicating to her mother that it was her turn. The mother shook her head no. Betsy could see the anxiety in her face, this strange girl with white skin suddenly in her home, asking her to drink a foul tasting liquid, demanding she give the unknown concoction to her precious child in her weakest, most vulnerable state.

Betsy looked compassionately at the little girl, helpless, skin covered in rashes. Her heart longed to help her. She placed her hand on the girl's chest and prayed silently, "Father in heaven, please let this little child be healed. Just has Jesus healed the sick, may you heal this girl. May these people see your great mercy and love for them. In Jesus name I pray, Amen."

When she finished the prayer, she felt the girl's chest rise up beneath her hand. The girl took a deep breath and opened her eyes. Instantly her mother was by her side, speaking to her in Maidu. Betsy withdrew to give them space. The girl looked better now that she was awake. Her eyes were bright and she had an energy Betsy had not expected. She was even smiling. She looked down at her arms and said something to her mother, and her mother, still on her knees, turned to Betsy. She was gushing thankfulness in words Betsy couldn't understand. Betsy was confused, she hadn't done anything to deserve such gratitude, and she began to back away. There was nothing more she could do now, she thought, but then the girl stood and raised her arms, shouting happily at Betsy. That's when Betsy saw...the rash was gone.

Betsy's eyes welled up with tears, those happy, joyful tears when you've witnessed something amazing, a moment of God's wonderful mercy and power. She stopped her retreat and stepped forward, embracing the mother. "God is good," was all Betsy managed to say. Then she got down on her knees in front of the little girl and gave her a big smile. "God is good," she said again.

It was a moment Betsy would remember forever. She let the feeling sink into her heart. She couldn't wait to tell her mom and dad, and Molly and Jack and...everyone! But she couldn't stay forever, so she gathered the cup and the pot and put her coat on. With a wave goodbye, she ducked out of the hut.

"Mom, you won't believe what happened in there," Betsy said.

"What happened?"

"I prayed and God just healed the little girl in there, just like that," she said, tears streaming down her cheeks.

"Oh, that's amazing!" said Mary, hugging her daughter. "I knew God wanted us to come here!"

Running-Water observed this conversation and leant his head into the hut again. He traded some words with the mother and then

179

looked at Betsy with a new respect and admiration. "You have strong medicine," he said in his broken English.

"No," responded Betsy. "Earth Creator has strong medicine!"

Joseph helped Running-Water understand. "He'lin Ka'keni," he said. Running-Water nodded.

Betsy wanted to make sure the Indians didn't think she had some special power. She wanted to make sure they knew it was God whose power was moving right in front of their eyes, first with words from her mouth and now with healing through her hand. Betsy only wished she knew Maidu so she could tell them more about the great healer, Jesus.

Betsy wondered if she could learn their language as they walked back towards the center of the village. There was only one bit of Maidu she knew, and she suddenly realized she could now find out its meaning. The words that had turned over and over in her mind, not stopping even when she was asleep, finally she could find out what they meant, what the bear woman had said.

She turned to Joseph and asked if he could translate. Then she spoke the words, "Hay'lin ko y'jen, e'muli ja k'ummeni y'jn."

"Where you hear these words?" asked Joseph.

"Kapam-Kylem spoke them to me. I've seen her before. Six days ago. I met her up on that ridge by accident," she said, pointing up to where her and her mother had left the horses. "She was riding a bear. I was very afraid. I've not forgotten those words. She was angry when she said them."

"Bear woman been angry for many years," said Joseph, "but now

180

she is angry no more. 'Hay'lin' means 'big' and 'ko' means 'snow.' 'Y'jen' means 'coming'. 'E'muli' means 'black,' 'Ja' means 'cloud' and 'k'ummeni' means 'winter'. Bear woman knew how to read the clouds."

Betsy pieced the words together, "Big...snow...coming, black...cloud...winter...coming." She thought for a moment. "She knew the storm was coming! Before it ever arrived!"

Betsy stopped walking. She realized the words of Kapem-kylem hadn't been directed at her, but they had been a warning. "But why was she so angry?"

"Bear woman once great healer. Her medicine was strong. But her anger grew when more and more white people came into our land. Then her medicine became weak. She blame white man for disturbing ka'kani. She said Hee'no angry, stole her medicine."

"What are ka'keni?" asked Betsy.

Joseph spread his arms to the sky to express his words. "Ka'kani sky people. Very powerful. Very old. Great spirits. Hee'no is coyote ka'kani. He is trouble-maker."

"I see why she was angry now," said Betsy. A sudden sadness swept over her. The old medicine woman had lost her power to heal. Having just experienced the joy of making people better, Betsy now felt the sadness of what the old woman had lost and what she'd been through.

"I wish our people and your people could just live together in peace," Betsy said sadly.

"Maidu people want peace. No make trouble. But trouble follow us, like hunter follow elk," said Joseph solemnly.

Betsy's mother joined the conversation, "Mr. Joseph, we do not wish to bring you any trouble. We came to offer our friendship and our good will. I'm deeply sorry for the death of Kapam-Kylem."

"You not kill Kapam-Kylem. Anger kill Kapam-Kylem," replied Joseph.

CHAPTER 21

THE ROAD HOME

§

There was a small gathering of Maidu in the center of the village when Betsy and Mary returned from the huts of the sick. They were gathered around the Christmas tree. They were talking animatedly, and Betsy smiled with the thought that at least her plan with the Christmas tree had worked.

Betsy and Mary joined the edge of the circle and Betsy said, "It's a gift, to you," and she made a motion of giving the tree to them.

Some of the Maidu nodded as if they understood, others looked confused. Then one of the men pulled a hunting knife from his belt and got down on one knee in front of the tree. He sliced the ropes that held it to the sled and the tree toppled over onto its side.

"Oh no," cried Betsy, and she ran to lift the tree back upright. The man who cut the ropes put his knife back and grabbed the sled. He held it out in front of him and inspected it. He nodded and smiled at Betsy.

"Oh sorry, no, that's not the gift," said Betsy, but her mother quickly put a hand on her shoulder and restrained her. She smiled at the men and motioned to them to keep it. All the Maidu smiled now.

"But Mom, that's Molly's..." whispered Betsy.

"Don't worry dear, I'm sure we can arrange to get her another."

Joseph leaned over and said, "My village thanks you for gift. They like it."

"The tree was supposed to be the gift," replied Betsy quietly.

Joseph responded in a whisper, "Dead tree not good gift."

Mary put her hand to her mouth to stifle a laugh. It would take Betsy a little longer to find that funny.

Suddenly a little girl came up to them. She was wearing an overcoat made of rabbit pelts, the fur on the inside and the skin on the outside. The villagers looked astonished and a murmur passed among them. Then Betsy realized what the villagers already knew - it was the little girl from the hut who only minutes before hadn't been able to get out of bed. What a shock it was to them to see her up and well!

The little girl extended her hands to Betsy, revealing a colorful necklace made of turquoise beads and white shells. It was a gift. Betsy got onto her knees and accepted it with a smile.

"It's beautiful," Betsy said. "Thank you. I will never forget this." Besty embraced the girl warmly, and again the Maidu smiled. Hugs, it seemed, were a gesture of good will no matter where you came from.

"What's your name?" asked Betsy, and Joseph translated.

"Okpa'jin," she replied with her little voice.

"It means sun ray," said Joseph.

"Can I visit you again, Oak-pa-jin?" asked Betsy. Again Joseph translated.

The little girl smiled and nodded.

The chief suddenly said some words, and everyone stopped to look at him. Betsy worried she'd said something wrong. He stepped forward in front of Mary and spoke loudly to her in his native language.

Joseph stepped in to translated, "He say thank you for bringing medicine to his people. He say you are a friend of the village."

The chief was wearing a chest piece that tied around his neck. It was made of rows of porcupine quills and decorated with red and orange beads. He removed this from his neck and presented it to Mary. Betsy's mother blushed and accepted the gift. She looked at it admiringly and then placed it around her own neck. The Maidu laughed at this, but the chief nodded his approval.

"Thank you for your kind words and your gift," she replied, with Joseph translating for all to hear. "The Earth Creator has brought us together today. He smiles from the heavens." The chief nodded solemnly, as did the rest of his tribe. Their respect for the Earth Creator was evident.

The chief spoke a few more words. Joseph translated, "Running-Water will go with you to road. I wish you safe journey home."

Then the chief nodded his farewell and turned away as Running-Water appeared to escort them out of the village. Betsy looked over at her Christmas tree laying neglected on its side. She motioned to Running-Water to take it with them, and he nodded his approval. She went to pick it up by the trunk, but Running-Water beat her to it and lifted it up onto his broad shoulder.

Besty and Mary waved to the Maidu as they left the village, crossing over the creek on a series of flat stones that had been arranged for the purpose. Running-Water knew an easier way up the ridge and the snow on this path had already been trampled down, but it was still quite a climb and they had to stop and rest a few times. When they did, they looked back over the snowy valley and down at the village below. Everyone had returned to their huts to warm themselves by their fires, and the smoke trails drifted up peacefully until the light wind caught them and carried them away. The sight was no longer a strange one, they had friends there now.

It took half an hour to make it back to the horses. Running-Water admired Sid and was surprised when it was Betsy who claimed the larger horse. If only she could tell him that story! He began to look for a way to lash the Christmas tree to the saddle, but Betsy stopped him. She removed from a sidebag what was left of the rope she'd use to tie it to the sled and handed it to him. Then she removed the popcorn garland so it wouldn't get any further damage. It was already looking rather rough having been battered by the journey both down into the village and back up again.

Running-Water managed to tie up the tree on the back of Sid, and then turned to face them. He pronounced, "Good-bye Mar-ee. Good-bye Bet-see."

"Goodbye Running-Water," they replied, and Mary followed it with, "See you again, friend." He turned and headed off back down the hill. Betsy and Mary climbed onto Sid and Tophat and they set off down the ridge in single file.

It was difficult riding downhill through the snow, and they didn't speak, but once they reached the road the going got easier, and they were able to ride side by side. Betsy was bursting at the seams to talk, and it all came out very rapidly when her mother finally pulled up next to her.

"Mom, can you believe what just happened?" spouted Betsy. "I don't think I even know what happened! I spoke Maidu! And then that little girl, Sun-Ray, what was her name? Oak-bar-kin? No, Oak-pa-jin. It was a miracle Mom! That rash was all over her arms and then just like that, it was gone! It's not possible is it? And, oh my, that Bear Woman! I can't believe she attacked you, I thought she was going to kill you, and then the earthquake, I just can't believe it!"

"Alright, alright, slow down a bit," urged her mother. "We have seen some amazing things today - real-life miracles. Your grandfather would be very proud! I'm going to write to him and tell him all about it. I haven't seen God work like that since I was your age and we had a revival."

"But did you ever hear anyone speak another language? That was crazy!" said Betsy, hardly able to contain herself.

"Yes, I *have* heard that before. You spoke in tongues, my dear one," assured her mother.

"Tongues?"

"Yes, tongues! You've read about it in the Bible."

"I have?"

"Yes my dear. In Acts. Don't you remember at Pentecost, when the Holy Spirit came down to the first church in Jerusalem? They began speaking in other languages, and those who didn't understand thought they'd had too much to drink!"

"Oh yes, I remember now..." recalled Betsy.

"It's a very special experience to be filled with the Holy Spirit and to let him speak through you. The Bible speaks of it quite often in the early church. It makes my skin tingle every time I witness it, though I must say it's been a long time. Too long!"

"Did your skin tingle back there?" asked Betsy.

"Oh yes," replied her mother, "very much so."

"Do you think it will happen again? I want it to, mom, it was so amazing! The feeling inside of me, it was so...peaceful and yet...energizing!"

"There's no saying, my dear, these things can't be forced. These things seem to happen to missionaries more than anyone else, and I suppose that is what we were today, missionaries."

"Maybe I'll be a missionary one day," mused Betsy.

"You already are, my dear, in a way. But we should not use the term lightly, it's a serious calling. If it is to be your life's work, then it requires lots of prayer and conviction. But I would not hold you back, my dear, it's in your blood after all."

"Do you think Grandpapa ever healed anyone?" asked Betsy.

"Many things happened in the revival when I was young. Healings, yes they happened, but what God did for that little girl back there was very special. I'm proud of you, Betsy, I'm proud that the Holy Spirit chose to move through you."

"I'm so glad we went, Mom. That was the best idea you've ever had!" gushed Betsy.

"God put it on my heart, my dear. All I had to do was listen and obey. We owe it all to Him. All, except the Christmas tree, that was your idea."

"Ma-ahm!" spouted Betsy indignantly. "I thought for sure they'd love it. But it all worked out in the end, now we can put it up in our house!"

"Oh, is that what you think?" laugher her mother. "Let's ask your father. It seems a rather strange thing to do, but at the same time it would be a shame to waste our hard work. It was rather pretty in the end."

They rode along in silence for a minute or so before Betsy mentioned the worst part, "Mom, I just don't know what to think of that Bear Woman. I was so afraid of her, and maybe rightly so, but now I feel bad she's dead."

"She was a woman worthy of fearing," replied her mother more seriously now. "I think she'd gone slightly mad. We can't see into the world of angels and demons, but if we could perhaps it would have been even scarier."

"You don't think we killed her, do you?" asked Betsy.

"Oh, no dear. We were defending ourselves. She was old and sick, and that rage she went into, well I suppose her body simply couldn't handle it."

"So you don't think it was God that struck her down then?"

"Oh, well, I think God decides when everyone should die. It was her time. But I don't think that was divine punishment. In the end she was a victim of her own anger."

"I wonder what will happen to her bear? You didn't even get to see it," said Betsy.

"Thank the Lord!" exclaimed her mother with a slight laugh. "One thing is for certain, God was in control the whole time, and when we follow Him, even though we should walk into the valley of the shadow of death, we fear no evil, for He is with us."

"Or slide into it..." said Betsy.

"Yes, or slide into it," said her mother. "You were very frightened by what happened the first time you met her, and for sure, it was a frightening thing. But you needn't let that control your life, not when God is with you."

"You're right, Mom," reflected Betsy. "I kinda got lost in my fear for a while there. I'm glad I had you to face it with me, though."

"Yes, sometimes we need each other, don't we?" said her mother comfortingly. "I'm not sure I could have done what you did back there, so I guess we need each other."

Betsy smiled. It seemed all her fears had been put to rest, and it was a good feeling to be heading home with her mother.

"Oh my goodness, what is Dad doing to say when I tell him I spoke in tongues?" laughed Betsy.

"I think he is going to be kicking himself for a long time for missing out," replied her mother.

CHAPTER 22

HOME

§

Betsy and her mother talked all the way home, and the journey went quickly. They dropped the horses off at Pete's stable and walked back, the Christmas tree held between them, through town towards home. The clouds had parted just as they'd arrived and the sun was getting low in the western sky, casting a beautiful warm light over the snow-covered mining town. The storm was finally over and blue skies had returned. It was a welcome sight.

Betsy was eager to see her father and hoped he was well enough to hear about their trip. She dropped the tree in front of their house, bounded up the front steps, threw open the front door, and, to her delight, found her father sitting in the front room.

"Oh Dad!" she exclaimed, running to hug him. "You won't believe what's happened!"

Reverend Wescott stood in an attempt to meet Betsy's flying embrace and almost fell back into the chair. "Oh, thank the Lord you're alright!"

Mary followed Betsy in and smiled to see her wrapped around

her father. She closed the door behind her, then froze and let out a little cry of surprise, which she muffled with her hand. There was a stranger sitting in the chair near the kitchen.

"Now Betsy, we have company," said the Reverend as she let go of him. She looked around and saw what she'd missed in her haste. There sat Jack Wilson with his black flat-brimmed hat in his hands. He seemed even larger now sitting there in the front room, broad shouldered and proud, his stern face set like stone.

He nodded at Betsy and said, "Hello Miss Betsy. Hello Mrs. Wescott."

"We've just been chatting," said her father. "He only just arrived. He got your telegram. I was just explaining that you'd left this morning to visit the Indian village and that I expected you back any time, and sure enough, here you are."

"Oh Mr. Wilson, it's so good of you to come," said Betsy apologetically. "We should have waited for you, but we didn't know if you'd get the telegram or when you'd get here."

"I am glad you come safely home. Please tell me - us," Jack corrected himself, "what happened."

Betsy launched into the story, starting with their attempt to find Joseph at the mining camp. She explained how they'd cut down a Christmas tree and decorated it, and how she'd entered the village by literally crashing into it. She told them how everyone had laughed when they'd seen what happened, and how the chief came out and didn't want their medicine. Then she told about the angry old Bear Woman, how she had attacked Mary and their struggle, and her tragic end.

Betsy told them about the earthquake and how the chief was convinced to allow them to use the medicine only after the Holy Spirit spoke through her using their native language. Her father asked lots of questions about this, amazed to hear that her daughter had spoken in tongues. Finally, she explained how she'd administered the medicine, and the healing of the little girl, Ok'pajin.

Throughout Betsy's recounting, her father would reel back in his chair with astonishment, and interject with "Is that right?" and "Well I'll be!" But Jack Wilson sat quiet and motionless, listening without comment.

It was getting dark outside by the time Betsy was finished and her Father had exhausted the last of his questions. The big Indian rose to his feet, and the three of them looked at him, waiting to hear what he had to say.

"I'm happy the Great Father kept you safe. You give good medicine to my brothers and sisters. We must always do good. That is what Great Father told me. I will go now," said Jack in his deep voice.

"Oh, not now! You must stay for dinner!" invited Betsy, her mother agreeing in the background.

"You send for help, I come. You no need my help, I go," said Jack Wilson.

Betsy stood quickly and intercepted him as he headed for the door. "I'm so sorry you came all this way for nothing," she apologized.

He stopped and looked down her very gravely. "Not for nothing. My vision was true. I saw the fight between angry Bear and brave Cougar. I saw mother fall as you watch, young Cub. I saw the earth shake and an Indian stop the fight. I heard the voice say 'Stop fighting!' The message from Great Father came to me and to Indian chief. Then I woke and come here. I rode horse hard and I spoke to Great Father hard. I beg Great Father: 'Protect Cougar. Protect Cub. Bring peace.' I say words over and over until I come here. Great Father heard my voice. He protect Cougar. He protect Cub. He bring peace. He healed Indian people. Good medicine comes from Great Father. Young cub, you not need me. Great Father is with you."

He set his big hand on Betsy's little shoulder and she saw for the very first time a thin smile appear on his face. Then he turned, placed his big black hat on his head, and went to retrieve his overcoat from the hook on the wall by the front door. Betsy's father and mother rushed to see him out.

"Thank you for your prayers, Mr. Wilson," said Mary.

Henry invited him to visit again. As he stepped out the front door he paused and looked down.

"There is dead tree on your porch," he said in confusion.

"It's a Christmas tree, Mr. Wilson," said Betsy cheerfully.

The big Indian shook his head and walked down the steps between piles of snow. Jack Wilson, the wood-cutter, Wovoka, disappeared down the street in the evening light, but even after he'd gone, the Wescotts could still feel something of him remaining with them, as if they'd been in the presence of a very special person.

194

"*Stop fighting*. That's exactly what the chief said," Betsy recalled in amazement. "I didn't mention that. How did Jack Wilson know that?"

"Us white folk don't have exclusive rights to God, Betsy. He can speak to anyone He pleases," said her Dad gently. "It seems Mr. Wilson had something of a vision from the Almighty. And God heard his prayers for your protection."

"Mr. Bao *did* say he was a prophet," mused Betsy.

"I think we're indebted to him," said her mother.

"I am twice over," realized Betsy. The strange Indian had saved her life not once, but two times now.

"Well, I don't know about you, but I'm starved," said her mother as she walked back to the kitchen.

"Dad, I have a small matter to ask you about. The Indians don't seem to care much for Christmas trees, what do you say we set the one on the porch up inside. Say, right over here?" proposed Betsy as she pointed to a spot by the front window. "I saved the garland, and you have no idea how long ma and I were up last night making it!"

"Where do you get these notions?" asked her Dad humorously.

"Oh, please father? After all we've been through today?" begged Betsy.

"Oh my, you're laying it on thick," said her Dad, laughing now.

"Only 'til Christmas," said Betsy.

Her father came over, looked her in the eyes, and smiled. "Of course my dear, it shall become a new tradition in the Wescott home.

By it we shall remember the great day God moved amongst the Indians of Rattlesnake Diggins."

Betsy couldn't get her mind to stop as she lay in bed that night. She just couldn't believe everything that had happened. She kept replaying it in her mind, savoring the parts where God had done amazing things…even making the ground shake!

Her mother cracked open her bedroom door and looked in on her. "Can't sleep?" she said.

"Not a wink," said Betsy.

Her mother came in and sat on the edge of her bed. "It was a pretty special day."

"Can we go back there soon?" asked Betsy.

"Yes, I think we should. God wouldn't want us to waste the miracles he worked now would He?"

"What do you mean?" asked Betsy.

"Well, Jesus did miracles to prove he was the Son of God, and I believe when God performs miracles in front of us, it's so that His glory would be known."

"I think they do know about God's glory, only they call him the Earth Creator," said Betsy. "Mom, how do we know we've got it right and they've got it wrong? About God, you know?"

"Who said they've got it wrong?" asked her mother.

"But they're not Christians," said Betsy.

"God has revealed himself to them in a different way," said her mother. "Their culture is much different than ours, but somehow they know there is an Earth Creator, just as we know there is a God."

"So does that mean when they die they'll go to heaven?" asked Betsy.

"Oh, well only God knows that. He's the judge," said her mother.

"But they don't know Jesus, mom. I thought he was the only way to heaven."

"That is true. No man comes to the Father except through Jesus, he said so himself. But did you ever think about all those people in the Old Testament? They didn't know Jesus, they only knew God. Some expected a Messiah, that is true, but not all. And yet Abraham, Moses, Noah, we know they went to heaven."

"That's true... But how?" asked Betsy.

"Well, they were faithful to God based on the way God chose to reveal himself to them."

"So it could be the same for the Indians?" asked Betsy.

"Only God can answer that, dear, not your mother. But I will tell you this, there is one way we can guarantee they will go to heaven, and that is by believing in Jesus. That is why we tell everyone we can about the good news of the Gospel."

"So is that why we're going back?" asked Betsy.

"Yes. God told us to go into the world and spread the good news. Your father and I believe that strongly. That's why he's a pastor and I'm his wife. And your grandfather believes the same. But you can't just walk up to an Indian, or anyone for that matter, and expect them to change everything they think about God and the world. We have to get to know them, understand them, love them, and then we can naturally share what has brought us so much joy."

Betsy thought about it and nodded to her mother. She always spoke such good sense. "I hope we can make friends with those Indians. I want to take Jack and Molly up to meet Skipping-Rock and Oak-pa-jin."

"I think that's a grand idea," said her mother. "Now I don't know about you, but I'm exhausted. I'm gonna go crawl into my own bed, and if I'm not up in the morning, don't you come wake me, you just help yourself to breakfast, alright my dear?"

"Alright ma," said Betsy, yawning. "You can go if you're that tired. But I'm not tired."

"Sure, dear, not you. Night-night," her mother said as she rose and slipped the door shut behind her.

The next day Betsy had to break the bad news about her sled to Molly. She was rather sad to lose it, even after Betsy had told her the whole grand story. However, Reverend Wescott spoke with Jack Fairlane Sr. to ask if he could make a replacement. Now Jack Sr. did not approve of what Betsy and Mary had done that day, he said it was 'foolhardy' and that they were lucky they didn't get themselves killed. But the Reverend spent much time lavishing praise on the convertible wagon-sleigh Jack Sr. was working on for Pete's winter runs down to Camptonville, and when the Reverend finally offered that the church would commission him a small sum for the new sled,

Jack Sr. could no longer refuse. In the end, his creation was far superior to the sled that had gone to the Indians: longer, faster, and, best of all, steerable. He was rather proud of it, and soon he had requests from every child in Downieville. He called it the Fairlane Flyer, and you can still buy one like it today.

Only one person was lost to the outbreak of scarlet fever that winter, thanks to the ancient Chinese medicine of Mr. Bao and God's mercy. All the miners recovered, as did the two Maidu families at Rattlesnake Diggins. Only Kapam-Kylem, the Bear Woman, died that winter, and whether the cause of death was fever, old age, or a bitter heart, no one could rightly say. The Maidu mourned her in the way that was customary for them – the Great Cry – and buried her near the village in her best clothes, adorned with strings of beads and feathers.

In the early spring Betsy and Mary returned to the village at Rattlesnake Diggins. Betsy became friends with Skipping-Rock and Ok'pajin, and they would share many laughs as Betsy tried to learn Maidu words, and they tried to learn English words.

One day she asked what became of Kapam-Kylem's old black bear. She learned the medicine woman had raised it from a cub, which had been abandoned when some of the tribe's men had hunted and killed its mother for meat and fur. Normally they wouldn't kill a mother bear, but they hadn't realized it until it was too late. The chief wouldn't let Kapam-Kylem bring the bear into the village, so she raised it up in the mountains where it had its own den. Some of the hunters knew where it was, and they checked it after she died, but they never found the bear.

Later in the year when summer came, Betsy took Molly and Jack to visit the village for the first time, and Jack was much affected. He eventually changed his ill-informed opinions of his native American neighbors. Mary got to know Joseph, and he introduced her to a few of the other adults. The village chief was most interested to speak with Mary again, and speak they did, but I suppose if I were to tell you all of what happened there I would need another book, and it's about time this one came to an end.

Betsy sometimes remembered the fear she'd felt in the face of that angry, old, white-faced medicine woman and the snarling muzzle of her big black bear, but she'd also learned how to let it go. That's not to say she was never scared again. We've read enough to know that Betsy's path through life would be much like that journey in the snowstorm: wide-open and exposed to the wildness of the natural world and to the wildness of all kinds of different people, good and bad. But in those moments of fear, she'd always remember what Jack Wilson had told her after that day up at Rattlesnake Diggins: The Great Father was with her. And she'd remember the verse her mother had showed her: perfect love drives out fear. All you need is a little love and you can slide right down into whatever it is your afraid of. One thing is for sure, the Great Father will be there.

THE END

HISTORICAL NOTE

WOVOKA

§

Unlike the imagined Bear Witch, Wovoka was a real person. Jack Wilson was a larger than life character much as described in our story. He was raised by Christians and later had his own distinctly native American spiritual experience that led him to become a medicine man and a "prophet." It is said he could predict storms and call rain when it was needed for crops and livestock, and there are accounts of him healing people with a white eagle feather and song-like prayers.

No one will ever know if Wovoka performed real miracles or if they were cleverly devised tricks. One of Wovoka's most impressive claims was that he was bulletproof. To demonstrate his invincibility, he would walk a few paces from a friend who held a gun, drop his blanket and stand in the middle of it. His friend would aim the gun and shoot him. Unperturbed, he would expose his shirt with holes in it and collect the shot from the blanket. It wouldn't be a difficult trick to conjure if the gun was loaded with a blank, and he'd cleverly concealed bullet up his sleeve.

One of his most famous "miracles" was making a block of ice

fall from the sky, but a skeptical witness claimed there was a rather large cottonwood tree above that could have concealed it until the proper time. Nonetheless, many believed he had control over the elements of nature, not just because of the block of ice, but because of the many instances when he'd made it rain.

Living in desert country, a drought could lead to the death of livestock. During one drought, he told a farmer he could make it rain if he'd share some of his beef with him. The farmer didn't believe him, but the drought got worse and his cows started dying. The farmer came back to Wovoka and said he'd give him some meat. Sure enough, Wovoka called the rain and down it came. The farmer was a believer after that, and kept him supplied with beef out of gratitude.

But the main calling of Wovoka was to spread a message of love and peace given to him by the Great Father in a vision. He was not educated and could not read or write, so he spread it by word of mouth at spiritual gatherings, much like prophets in the Bible, but in the context of his ancient Paiute culture. The native American's spirituality was practiced through dances around a fire, usually in a large hut. Wovoka spoke a strong message during these dances: make peace with your brother and with the white man, always be honest and work hard.

So it seems Wovoka was equal parts prophet and trickster. No doubt he was a faulted human being, just like all of us. His religion might seem strange to modern Christians, but we should not leave out the possibility that God chose to work through a man like Wo-voka.

Someone once asked Wovoka how he could make it rain. His response was written down and later recounted and recorded by a historian:

"I'll tell you, my boy. You can do it. Anybody can do it. But you'll have to have love, special love. Big love for the Great Messiah. And if you love the Great Messiah with all your mind, your body and your spirit, he will show you many things of the mystery of the earth. And if you believe in him with all your spirit, when the land dries up, if you believe that there is a Great Messiah, when the water dries up and there will be no water, He will give you the power..."[1]

Near the end of his life, Wovoka predicted that he would shake the earth if he ever saw heaven again. Exactly three months from the day of his death, the valley in which he was buried recorded the most powerful earthquake of the time. The noble man's vision of heaven had finally come true.

---

[1] Michael Hittman (1990), Wovoka and the Ghost Dance, University of Nebraska Press. The author would like to thank Mr. Hittman for his invaluable research on Wovoka, which informed much of the fictional account of the man given in this story.

ABOUT THE AUTHOR

In his adventurous days, Aaron Neumann travelled all around the world and spent years in faraway lands, but now he has settled into a peaceful, contented life in the green and fertile lands of Ohio with his two lovely daughters and his beloved wife. By day he works as a scientist in the art of wheeled motion, but come lunch time he sneaks away to a secret spot where he sits on a big rock amidst a burbling creek to read books and write stories. He enjoys escaping to the woods whenever he can, even in the worst of winter. And when the snow flies, there is a good chance you'll find the whole Neumann clan frolicking and sliding down snow-covered hillsides, just like Betsy and her friends.